PENGUIN MODERN CLASSICS
Ha Ha Hu Hu

VISWANADHA SATYANARAYANA (1895–1976) is regarded as one of the most important writers and poets of the Telugu canon. He was the first Telugu writer to win the Jnanpith Award in 1971. He was also awarded the Padma Bhushan.

VELCHERU NARAYANA RAO is a renowned scholar and translator. His previous translations include, among many others, Gurajada Apparao's *Girls for Sale* and Chaso's *Doll's Wedding* (with David Shulman), both for Penguin Classics.

PRAISE FOR THE BOOK

'The short works translated and presented in this book are small yet sparkling gems, the works of an important, highly prolific and original author in twentieth-century Telugu, Viswanadha Satyanarayana. In turn, it takes a bold scholar like Velcheru Narayana Rao to do justice to the complex, and subtle, vision of a maverick like Satyanarayana. These works, written in a droll and ironic tone, should be widely read, and help to bring Satyanarayana the large audience that he truly merits.' SANJAY SUBRAHMANYAM

VISWANADHA SATYANARAYANA

Ha Ha Hu Hu

A HORSE-HEADED GOD IN TRAFALGAR SQUARE

Translated from the Telugu with an Introduction
and Afterword by Velcheru Narayana Rao

PENGUIN BOOKS

An imprint of Penguin Random House

PENGUIN BOOKS

USA | Canada | UK | Ireland | Australia
New Zealand | India | South Africa | China | Singapore

Penguin Books is part of the Penguin Random House group of companies
whose addresses can be found at global.penguinrandomhouse.com

Published by Penguin Random House India Pvt. Ltd
4th Floor, Capital Tower 1, MG Road,
Gurugram 122 002, Haryana, India

Vishnu Sharma Learns English first published in Telugu as *Vishnu Sharma
Inglīshu Caduvu* by author, Vijayawada circa 1961
Ha Ha Hu Hu first published in Telugu by author, Vijayawada circa 1932
First published in Penguin Books by Penguin Random House India 2018

Copyright © Viswanadha Satyanarayana circa 1961, 1932
English translation, introduction and afterword © Velcheru Narayana Rao 2018

ISBN 9780143426226

For sale in the Indian Subcontinent only

Typeset in Adobe Caslon Pro by Manipal Digital Systems, Manipal

Printed at Repro India Limited

www.penguin.co.in

This is a legitimate digitally printed version of the book and therefore might not
have certain extra finishing on the cover.

For
Venkateswara Rao Veluri
and Shanti Veluri,
remembering decades of friendship

Contents

Introduction

Viswanadha Satyanarayana: A Different Postcolonial

Colonialism came to India with a complex interlocking of Western modernity and British political control. The Enlightenment ideas of rational thinking, egalitarianism, linear history and the grand knowledge of science that conquers nature to enhance human happiness—all came in the wake of colonialism, giving Western civilization the look of a boon conferred upon India by the colonial master. Nationalists rejected colonial political control but were unwilling to give up the modernity that came with it. This position is best presented by Dipesh Chakrabarty:

> Concepts such as citizenship, the state, civil society, public sphere, human rights, equality before the law, the individual, distinctions between public and private, the idea of the subject, democracy, popular sovereignty,

social justice, scientific rationality, and so on all bear the
burden of European thought and history. One simply
cannot think of political modernity without these and
other related concepts that found a climactic form in
the course of the European Enlightenment and the
nineteenth century.[1]

Writers in India during the colonial period who were largely
nationalistic were opposed to British governance, but were
reluctant to reject the modern literary culture that entered
the Indian literary world via the English language. In all
of India's literary languages a new divide developed under
the influence of the English language—a divide baptized
by its promoters with such words as *ādhunika*, or *navya*,
which broadly indicated an awareness of a new beginning,
a modernity. Acceptance of the modern also inaugurated a
defiance of literary practices that had held sway until then.
Modern poets wrote on contemporary themes, with a liberal
agenda. They were against caste hierarchies, superstitious
rituals of religion, Brahmin superiority; some of them were
clearly in favour of class war and revolution. There were very
few who did not buy into a social reformist agenda, which
was largely considered a mark of modernity. From Bankim
Chandra Chattopadhyay to Tripuraneni Gopichand,
from Rabindranath Tagore to Sumitranandan Pant,
from Subrhamanya Bharati to Sri Sri, all major modern
writers and poets followed this general trend. Viswanadha
Satyanarayana in Telugu, not well known outside India, is
one among a minority who does not belong in this group.

Satyanarayana and His Times

Born in 1895 in a Vaidiki Brahmin family, Satyanarayana received his early education in village schools called 'street schools'. His village education gave him roots in a local culture of street singers, dancers, Purana performers—singers from castes now called Dalits—itinerant tellers of religious stories and oral poets. His elder sister sang songs for him, told folk tales, and taught stories from the Ramayana and the Mahabharata, and other old texts. The temple carnival that occurred annually attracted actors, musicians who played various instruments, clowns, wrestlers, magicians and performers who took different guises. In his village, people of all castes used to call each other by kinship terms—brother, sister, uncle and aunt—despite divisions imposed by caste regulations. According to Satyanarayana's recollection, he grew up in a certain idyllic environment of a large joint family that shared love and affection, songs and stories. As an innocent young boy, he internalized the apparent love in the village, perhaps unrealistically free from the strife and struggle, conflict and corruption that only an adult could see.

By the time Satyanarayana was eleven, his father, who was a little too generous for his own good, gave away most of his ancestral property. He decided that his son should get an English education to make a living, and the family moved to the nearby town of Machilipatnam. When he saw that his son was writing Telugu poetry, he commanded him not to waste his time in such futile

activities. Satyanarayana continued to write poetry anyway,
though he tore up thousands of his early verses. Too poor
to buy books for himself, he sat and read at a bookstore.
The owner had a kind heart and allowed him to read the
books he wanted, and even borrow them overnight. While
pursuing his English education, Satyanarayana learnt
traditional sastra texts from various individual scholars.
He learnt Tarka (logic) and Vyākaraṇa (grammar), and
Vedanta (philosophy) from the great scholars of the time,
Kambhampati Ramamurti Sastri, Parimi Ramanarasimha
Sastri and Kanukolanu Trivikramarama Rao—scholars
whose names are mostly forgotten now. For Telugu
poetry, Satyanarayana became a student of the great poet
Chellapilla Venkata Sastry (1870–1950).[2]

By the 1920s Satyanarayana was recognized as a major
voice in Telugu literature. His turns of phrase and his
inventiveness in Sanskrit compound formation attracted the
attention of many readers and gave him a place among noted
writers. He was nationalistic and patriotic in his early poems,
singing the greatness of past Telugu kings and empire
builders. The topics were predictable, but his phrases were
striking and distinguished him from a host of other patriotic
poets. In the 1940s, when every modern writer considered
the Ramayana a text only suitable for old people who read
it for religious merit, Satyanarayana began to compose a
six-volume Ramayana in defiance of every modern literary
convention established by his contemporaries.

While the modern writers spoke of romantic love,
elevated the status of women and quoted from Shelley,

Keats and Eliot, Satyanarayana spoke of Brahminic dharma, which was in turn closely interconnected in literature with the Indian aesthetics of *rasa, aucitya, vakrokti* and *dhvani,* and quoted from Abhinavagupta, Mammata and a variety of *Alamkāra* texts from Sanskrit. This was a language modern writers had rejected some forty years earlier. The tradition reflected in this language was almost dead. Kandukuri Viresalingam (1848–1919) attacked upper-caste traditional practices with his social reform agenda. C.R. Reddy (1880–1951) condemned literary practices for their excessive attention to eroticism. Literary standards that had held sway for several centuries were fast losing ground. The juggernaut of modernity dominated the field and everything else appeared outdated and regressive. A modern group of poets, who called their poetry Bhava Kavitvam, openly defied pandits, and the standards of old poetry. Soon the Marxists would appear on the stage to call for revolutionary poetry addressed to the masses, and to reject all Telugu poetry up to that time as feudal and regressive.

During the early decades of the twentieth century, traditional learning which had been taught by pandits began to decline. These pandits, who were institutions unto themselves, taught their students in their homes, often giving them food and shelter. Otherwise the students, who were always Brahmins, found Brahmin houses in the locality who would give them food one day of the week. Seven such houses took care of their needs and the students spent many years studying with their teacher. The pandits themselves were supported by the zamindars of the area. The best of the students later went on to study in Kasi (Varanasi) or Navadvipa in Bengal, where greater pandits taught higher texts. This system which had maintained learning of such subjects as Tarka (logic), Vyākaraṇa (grammar) and Mimāmsa (hermeneutics) for a long time gradually died for lack of support.

Modern education in English—and other Western subjects such as history, mathematics, physics and chemistry—was available at the government-run high schools, colleges and universities, that awarded school certificates, and BA and MA degrees. Students who acquired such degrees landed lucrative jobs in the colonial bureaucracy. Telugu and Sanskrit were also taught at these institutions, but not with the same care as modern subjects taught in the medium of English. A two-tier system of faculty existed in these new schools: one group, who had degrees from colleges and universities, were called lecturers and professors; the other group, who held diplomas from what were called Oriental Colleges, in Sanskrit and Telugu and with little or no knowledge of English, were called pandits.[3] Lecturers and professors were paid higher salaries, while pandits were poorly paid. They even dressed differently. Pandits wore traditional clothes: a *dhovati* tied around the waist with a closed coat, head clean-shaven except for a tuft of hair, a *pilaka*, hanging behind and a religious *bottu* marking the forehead. Lecturers and professors were dressed in Western-style clothes, a shirt and slacks, with a jacket and tie and short hair. Even if the lecturers and professors occasionally wore a dhovati, they never shaved their heads or grew a pilaka. Almost every subject was taught in English, while Telugu, considered a second language, was treated as optional. It was very clear to the students that English and the subjects taught in it led them to a better future. Usually, students did not even attend their Telugu classes regularly, and when they did, they often made fun of their Telugu pandit, his pilaka and his manner of speech. They laughed and coughed and made animal noises in class. They badgered the pandit with embarrassing questions about words and passages describing a woman's body and lovemaking in old Telugu texts. The frustrated authorities who prescribed texts for study took care not to assign material that included explicitly erotic passages—even relatively harmless literary selections had references to women's breasts, nipples, thighs, buttocks and coitus, all of them in old Telugu or Sanskrit words for which the male students insisted on being given modern Telugu equivalents. The male students would manage to embarrass the young women in the same class, though on separate rows of benches, with mischievous questions addressed to the teacher.

In these schools, the life of a Telugu pandit was miserable. His general image was of a fossilized, unimaginative individual who somehow had instant access to all the old books he had memorized, but lacked the intelligence to study any modern subject. Nevertheless, the few students who had developed a taste for old Telugu and Sanskrit texts respected their Telugu teachers, and the

more impressive and dominating personalities among the
pandits possessed a presence that commanded respect. In
general, granting the exceptions, the status of the Telugu
teacher both in the eyes of the administrators and in the
eyes of the students was not high. The situation was
accepted with no protest. Poet Chellapilla Venkata Sastry
wrote in a matter-of-fact way:

> *tĕlugu caduv'aṭanna telikagā jūcu*
> *ṭ'āāṅgla pāṭhaśālaḷ'andu galadu.*

> That's how it is, they take Telugu lightly
> In all those English schools.[4]

By English schools he meant the schools in which all
subjects, except Telugu, were taught in the medium of
English. (Until the turn of the twentieth century, even
questions in Telugu examinations were set in English.)[5]

British officers of the department of education, who did
not know any Telugu, supervised Telugu instruction. In one
such instance, an officer observed a Telugu pandit use an
entire class period to teach a single verse in the old-fashioned
way, going through every word, explaining the compound
(*samāsa*), expanding the compound into a sentence (*vigraha
vākya*), showing the rules of *sandhi* and the figures of speech
(*alaṅkara*), and finally having the students sing the verse out
loud. The British inspector wrote a comment that it was
a waste of time to give all that detail and the class should
be speeded up. It was experiences such as this that made

Venkata Sastry bemoan the sins of his past life that had made him a Telugu instructor in such schools. Bhamidipati Kameswara Rao, a humourist in the early 1940s, wrote an essay describing the indignities Telugu instructors suffered in schools and colleges:[6] The word pandit, which was once a title of honour, suffered a semantic shift and now meant a poorly paid Telugu instructor.[7] It is an interesting contradiction that the Telugu pandit lost his status in society, even as Telugu was being extolled as a great language and the Telugu middle class agitated for a distinct identity from the Tamils with whom they shared an administrative unit—the Madras Province.[8]

In contrast, Telugu poets and pandits of the past centuries had enjoyed legendary support from kings who gave them rent-free land and gold and other valuables in return for dedicating their books to them. Ministers and leaders of the army and cavalry and even village heads patronized poets. Prefaces of books written by poets from the eleventh-century Nannayya onward tell glorious stories of such patronage. Legends of great kings such as Krishnadevaraya of the sixteenth century and Vijayaraghavanayaka of the seventeenth century are remembered by poets who celebrated them in song and verse. The British rulers did not care to emulate such practices, but the zamindars who were mostly tax farmers, attempting to embellish themselves with the trappings of past kings, tried to carry on the tradition of literary patronage to the extent they could. However, by the twentieth century even such patronage was waning. Poet Chellapilla Venkata Sastry described the

sorry state of traditional scholars during the early decades
of the twentieth century as follows:

> They read proofs at printing presses
> taught Telugu to the *hūna*s,[9]
> gave discourses on Vedanta for merchants
> who gave groceries on credit.
> Monumental scholars lived miserable lives just to stay alive.
> Respect for learning was lost.[10]

Traditional scholars who lost confidence in their learning
gradually began to accept the Orientalist construction of
traditional texts, and began to speak a confused language of
modern textual criticism and historical location of authors.
They accepted the standards of Western philology and
positivist literary history—two approaches unsuitable to
the nature of the Indian text. Furthermore, they accepted
the notions of Victorian morality and began to see the
eroticism of precolonial Indian literature as immoral. Later
on, Marxist notions that found acceptance among the
modern Indian intellectuals led them to declare such erotic
literature to be feudal, written for the carnal pleasures of
ruling kings and not for the masses. Thus, a formidable
group of people from modern poets to Marxists began to
militate against Satyanarayana and his literary work.

Marginalization of Sanskrit and old Telugu in the
academy created a new intellectual who confidently
assumed that old texts belonged to an age of ignorance.
Pandits who read them or people who quoted from them

were considered out of date, except those who quoted from such texts with a sprinkle of English from their Orientalist translations. Modern intellectuals read English poets and Western philosophers, thought in English, and even wrote their personal letters, notes, diaries and journals in English. Their interest in traditional literature was based on political and social ideologies rather than on literary sensibilities and modes of representation. A modern writer had to reject caste, avoid erotic descriptions, deny religious superstition, and depict progressive ideas about women and the pain suffered by lower castes in the hands of upper-caste Brahmins. Since Satyanarayana did not fit this bill, he was securely classed as feudal and a retrograde.

Satyanarayana was stereotyped as a defender of Vedic culture, backward looking and opposed to change. In a play depicting contemporary literary personalities, Tenneti Suri, a novelist and poet, represents Satyanarayana entering the stage brandishing his pen as a sword, and singing a poem written by Satyanarayana himself. The poem is from one of his mythological plays, *Venarāju*, where king Pṛthu, engaged in fighting against the anti-Vedic rule of king Vena, enters the stage singing this verse. In Suri's play, the poem becomes the battle cry of Satyanarayana himself. The poem in jaw-breaking Sanskrit compounds goes breathlessly as follows:

ati-mano-budhyahaṅkṛtul aupanisadu l
ātta-gaṇḍūṣita-trayul aurva-vahni

garbhitântah tapaskulu ghanulu ṛṣulak
ĕvvaḍu virodhi tadvadhak ĕttina yadī[11]

Beyond the mind, intellect or ego,
they personify the Upanishads and hold the three Vedas
in their full-throated voices, fierce
with the submarine fire in the depths
of their inner self—
they are the seers, the wise men,
the greats.
Anyone who dares to oppose them,
I'll kill him.

The high-voltage Sanskrit compounds in the poem and the energetic combinations of its phonemes create an atmosphere of fury and rage. The opening vowels of the first three phrases /a/ and /au/ and the long /ā/, followed by another diphthong and a compound that follows with the difficult consonantal cluster of /hni/, and a repetition of /ta/, one of them with a *visarga*, makes you almost breathless, but before you have a chance to catch your breath, the poem relentlessly demands utterance of an aspirate /gh/ and does not allow you to stop before you go on with the clause that ends with *ĕvvaḍu virodhi*, to complete the sentence in the last line. This one-sentence poem came to represent Satyanarayana in his battle with modern values.

Satyanarayana's formidable scholarship was matched by his monumental imagination and creative energy. He took Telugu poetry to unprecedented heights using mythological themes and writing in a classical style, but with compelling modern sensibilities. Boldly challenging those critics who argued against traditional values and traditional poetry, Satyanarayana took the less popular position, arguing that it was English education that made Telugu poets and intellectuals lose their heritage and their traditional excellence. Defying the fashionable modern political position that old epics, like the Ramayana, were detrimental to the progress of society, he wrote in the preface to his six-volume *Rāmāyaṇa Kalpavṛkshamu* (Ramayana, the Heavenly Tree):

> You ask, 'Why yet another Rāmāyaṇa?'
> In this world,
> everyone eats the same rice every day,
> but the taste of your rice is your own.
> People make love, over and over, but only you
> know how it feels. I write about the same Rāma
> everyone else has known, but my feelings of love
> are mine. Ninety per cent of what makes a poem
> is the genius of the poet. Poets in India know
> that the way you tell the tale
> weighs a thousand times more
> than some facile, novel theme.[12]

This kind of defence that Satyanarayana mounted to protect himself from the attacks of his opponents did not help. The attacks continued with the old school defending his *Rāmāyaṇa Kalpavṛkshamu* and the new-school poets

ridiculing it for its archaic diction and outmoded ideas.
Literary journals as well as daily newspapers encouraged
debate between these factions, which widened the breach
between them even more.[13] Satyanarayana's detractors
created a caricature of his literary person as one who looks
back and opposes every social and political change.

Satyanarayana's lifestyle and the way he dressed
bolstered this caricature. He looked like a traditional
Brahmin, wearing a dhovati and a *kaṇḍuvā* (upper cloth
on the shoulder) in the old pandit style, as well as a
bottu on his forehead. In contrast, the Bhava Kavitvam
poets wore their *pañcĕ* and *lālci* in the Bengali style
popularized by the followers of Tagore, sported long,
curly hair hanging down to their shoulders and wore
gold-rimmed glasses, while the Marxist poets wore slacks,
shirts and had short hair. Even in the way they dressed,
each group of poets looked as though they belonged
to different worlds. Satyanarayana's scholarship and
language were also held out for ridicule. His detractors
laughed at him for his preference for difficult, arcane
words that even the most erudite scholars could not
follow. Popular magazines lampooned him in cartoons
and jokes.[14]

One of his admirers, Jalasutram Rukmininatha Sastri,
even wrote a parody playfully imitating Satyanarayana's
style:

> *kiñcittikta-kashāya-shāḍaba-rasa-kshepâti-rekâti vāk*
> *sañcāra-pracayâvakāśamulalo kavyudhgha!*

gaṇḍāśmamul cañcallīlan udātta vāggarmiato sādhiñci
  vedhincumā
pañcāriñci pravahlikā kṛta kṛtin, pāshāṇa-pāka-prabhū!

Torture us, please,
impossible poet,
with your exuberance of stunning words
and delicious feeling slightly mixed
with bitter dryness. We need jaws of stone
to grind the elevated phrases you utter with ease
as you tease us through your labyrinths,
books cooked to the texture of rock.[15]

The vocative with which Rukmininatha Sastri ends his
poem—*pāshāṇa-pāka-prabhū*—master of rock-hard-style,
became a nickname for Satyanarayana that both his friends
and foes used.[16]

But Satyanarayana had his answer to his critics. He
wrote in response:

In the old days, if a text was demanding,
the reader felt it was *his* lack.
These days the poet is to blame.
Devious are the ways
of this dying age.[17]

The original words for 'this dying age' were 'the age of Kali'
in the Puranic chronology of four yugas, during which time
progressively deteriorates and runs in a downward spiral.

Satyanarayana refused to use the linear time of the Christian calendar.

In contrast to his vociferous critics, Satyanarayana's admirers elevated him to the status of one of the greatest poets in the history of Telugu literature. They called him the very incarnation of the goddess Sarasvati. Most of his admirers came from old-fashioned Brahmin families, learned in old Telugu and Sanskrit—two subjects that were losing ground among the younger generation. In this fierce clash of cultures, where the lines were drawn somewhat uncritically, Satyanarayana's anti-colonial message was lost in the din of attacks and counter-attacks. Modernists saw in Satyanarayana's critique of colonialism a move to revive Brahmin superiority and a step back to a society riddled with superstition and ignorance that every social reformer in India from Raja Rammohun Roy to Viresalingam had fought against.

If Satyanarayana's social programme was difficult for his critics to support, his literary presence was too powerful to ignore. He was not easily marginalized as an old pandit. He was too modern to be outdated and too outdated to be modern. He was everywhere—as a writer, critic, public intellectual and a formidable opponent of everything the new middle class stood for. For about half a century, he walked the Telugu literary scene like a four-hundred-pound gorilla in the living room who could not be ignored.

In the 1930s, Satyanarayana wrote his major novel, *Veyi Paḍagalu (A Thousand Hoods)*, a one-thousand-page tome, in which he advocated with relentless energy his vision of an India free from colonial cultural domination. He went on to write a large number of novels in which he represented his characters fighting a losing battle against the modernity of what he called the Kali age—his name for the present times. In the 1940s, his novel *Cĕliyalikaṭṭa* (Sister's Limit) countered a powerful novel by a radical writer, Gudipati Venkata Chalam (1894–1979), who vigorously advocated for sexual and social freedom for women. Chalam's novel *Maidānam* (Open Land) depicts a Brahmin woman who leaves her lawyer-husband and elopes with a young Muslim man; they live a life of sex, love and joy away from people in an open, uninhabited, land free from the norms of society. Satyanarayana's novel, in contrast, poses the problem of rejecting society. The name of the novel, *Cĕliyalikaṭṭa*, is based on the popular belief that the ocean never crosses its limit, its shore, to submerge the area where people live, because the shore represents the ocean's sister, and 'crossing' it would amount to incest. Only when something violently destructive to the moral order happens, does the ocean cross its boundary and destroy towns and villages.

In his late sixties, Satyanarayana undertook a massive publishing contract to write twelve novels—under the series heading of *Purāna Vaira Grantha Māla*, (Garland of Books Depicting the Ancient Battle between Good and Evil). In his world view, there is a continuing battle between the divine forces and the demonic forces in the world in every age. His responsibility is to show in these novels how the demonic forces are vigorously waging the battle again in the present Kali age and how they will be eventually defeated.

For all the traditionalism of his literary works, the social values he professed and his style of dressing like a Brahmin pandit, Satyanarayana was known to his friends to have been very modern in his private life. His biography is yet to be written, but close associates say that he was an avid reader of English novels, a devoted viewer of English movies, and enjoyed life to the fullest with a vigour unheard of among the restrictive Vaidiki Brahmins.

Friends speak of him as a very loving and affectionate person but known to be rather harsh in his words, easily misunderstood by people. He even made enemies of people who admired him. Uncompromising in his tastes, he was deeply distressed by shallow learning and superficiality. He often yelled at people who admired him for the wrong reasons. He was very confident of his strengths and talents to the extent that he gave the impression of excessive pride. He was reluctant to praise potential patrons even during the times when he was poor. A telling incident reported by friends is the following: Vikramadeva Varma, the maharaja of Jaipur (1869–1951), who was himself a poet and enjoyed being a patron of poets, was honouring Telugu poets in Eluru. Poets big and small came and read their verses and received an award of one hundred and sixteen rupees. When poet after poet went up to the stage and received the award, Chellapilla Venkata Sastry, Satyanarayana's teacher, encouraged Satyanarayana to go up and read some verses as well. Satyanarayana was badly in need of money and one hundred and sixteen rupees was a lot of money in those days. Satyanarayana stood up and read the following poem:

A boy was born
like a true wish-giving tree
in the palace of gold, studded with precious gems.
Millions celebrated
and nuggets of gold were given away
as gifts, courtesans danced
music of joy played;
the whole world rejoiced.

A poet was born in a poor family.
The midwife complained she was not given
enough food,
while the Brahmin muttered a few chants.

The royal child grew
to be a handsome prince,
proud like a galloping horse,
adorned with gems and jewels.
The little poet shrivelled in hunger
life blinking faint in his eyes.

Trees bent and shaded the prince
when he was tired in his travels.
The child poet was scorched in the heat
of the sharp rays of a piercing sun.

The day when a full life of extended luxury ended,
for the king
trumpets sounded again,
and the Vedic chants sounded like
the thunder of rain clouds.

That evening from the sky,
in a brilliance
of a finely cut diamond
a star fell down to earth.

The poet's life of pain and suffering ended,
the sun went down as his body was consumed in flames.
As it was getting dark,
spreading a new brilliance,
a star climbed up to the firmament.[18]

Despite his ideas and opinions, and despite the strong and sometimes vicious attacks of his critics, Satyanarayana's books sold; he was perhaps the only author in Telugu who lived mostly on the income from his books. This was not necessarily because of a well-established market for books. Satyanarayana lived at a time when the publishing industry was not well developed. He published his own books, while a new group of middle-class donors, who continued the old zamindari style of patronizing poets and scholars, supported him. He dedicated his books to his new patrons and they paid for the printing costs. In the front part of the book he wrote verses praising the patrons and often described their families very much in the way old poets did.[19] But in every such instance, he kept his position higher than that of his patron, as one who bestowed a blessing on them rather than one who received support from them. Some of Satyanarayana's books were dedicated to his friends, out of love for them, and many of the verses he wrote in that context became memorable for their sharp wit, like the one he wrote addressing the great historian Mallampalli Somasekhara Sarma, as a scholar 'born at a miserable time when learning without a college degree has no value'. It was common knowledge in Andhra that Sarma had done pioneering work on the history of pre-modern Andhra kings, painstakingly deciphering and piecing together information from rock inscriptions and copperplates, but he was never hired as faculty by any university since he did not have a degree in history. Quoted on many occasions in public gatherings and private get-togethers, these and several other dedicatory verses of Satyanarayana entered the public space of *cāṭu* oral tradition.

A Personal Note

My acquaintance with Satyanarayana dates from about 1950, when I was taking a break from my studies, doing odd jobs, hanging out with poets and scholars, and reading whatever interested me. During those years and later I visited Satyanarayana several times—it was easy to see him because he lived in Vijayawada, a town some sixty kilometres south of Eluru, where I lived, and because he was very approachable. At the time, I was deeply influenced by Marxist literary theories and was a great admirer of Sri Sri, who immensely influenced my generation with his revolutionary poetry. Most of my friends and acquaintances with whom I spent time reading and discussing Marx and Mao were not initiated into old Telugu literature enough to even admit Satyanarayana into their company. Reading French, German and Italian poets and writers was fun— Sartre, Heine, Pirandello, Kafka and Unamuno, kept us up late into the night; but my taste for Satyanarayana intrigued the group. They suffered my passion and even enjoyed his verses when I sang for them and they seemed to see that there was something worthwhile in his poetry, though it was too arcane for them. To find some comfort, I had to go to another group of somewhat older pandits, who did not know anything of Western literature, and who were steeped in Telugu and Sanskrit. I lived in two worlds—each incompatible with the other, and each unmindful of the other. My modernist friends mildly tolerated my passion for Satyanarayana, my Marxist friends did not understand why I read this arch-reactionary, and my pandit friends did not care for my admiration for the Marxist poets, who they believed were not poets at all. I kept reading Satyanarayana, and as the years passed, my understanding of his work deepened, even as I found myself violently opposing his social and political views. There was one occasion when he and I met on the same public stage, when he defended the sages and classical poets, and I spoke vigorously, in my youthful enthusiasm, in support of the Marxist poets and their philosophy of revolutionary change. My respect for him never diminished and I continued to see a modern poet in him, while his admirers saw him only as a defender of tradition.

After I moved to the United States, I met with Satyanarayana several times. I asked for his permission to translate some of his work into English, which he gladly encouraged me to do. It was my failure that I did nothing before he died in 1976. In 2002, I included a few selections from his poems in my edited volume, *Twentieth Century Telugu Poetry: An Anthology*, some of which I translated with David Shulman, who shares my admiration and understanding of Satyanarayana.[20]

This volume contains two novellas, *Ha Ha Hu Hu: A Horse-Headed God in Trafalgar Square* and *Vishnu Sharma Learns English*. The dates of these novellas are uncertain. Compilers of his bibliography report that *Ha Ha Hu Hu: A Horse-Headed God in Trafalgar Square* was written in 1932, but his son thinks it was 1952. *Vishnu Sharma Learns English* was published as a book in 1961, but at an earlier uncertain date it came out serially in *Krishna Patrika*.[21] This translation is a modest, somewhat belated, attempt to introduce Satyanarayana to English-reading audiences with a hope that it might encourage a closer study of his works.

Ha Ha Hu Hu: A Horse-Headed God in Trafalgar Square

This is the story of a *gandharva*, a mythological character from the Puranas. Gandharvas are a class of semi-divine beings who have the head of a horse, a human body and wings. Flying through the sky, the gandharva falls into Trafalgar Square in London and loses consciousness. People gather around this huge 'animal' and start wondering what it could be. Police surround the animal and build a cage around it to prevent it from hurting anyone. The gandharva wakes up and starts speaking Prakrit. Nobody understands what this strange animal is doing, nor can they make sense of the sounds it makes. From up close, the sounds are too loud to hear as anything more than noise. Sanskrit professors from London University, who are listening from a distance and who can hear clearly because of the distance, recognize that the animal is speaking a language close to Sanskrit. They try to speak to him in Sanskrit and ask, 'What did you say?' The animal responds in perfect Sanskrit: *atra samīpe asti vā kaschinnadī—snātumicchāmi.* 'Is there a river nearby, I want to take a bath.' That's how the story begins.

Vishnu Sharma Learns English

The second novella, *Vishnu Sharma Learns English*, is equally inventive. A thirteenth-century Telugu poet, Tikkanna, who wrote the Mahabharata in Telugu, and Vishnu Sharma, a Sanskrit scholar, who wrote the *Pancatantra*, a book of statecraft believed to have been written at some ancient date, appear in the dream of a Telugu lecturer in a small Andhra town, Vijayawada (now a relatively big city), on the east coast of south India, and want to learn English from him. Indra, the king of the gods, and the ruler of heaven, has sent them. The novella is written as a series of dreams in which the instructor and his new students engage in hilarious conversations, with a stunning ending.

Note on Translating the Novellas

Satyanarayana dictated his novels to scribes. He rarely wrote himself. He often dictated very short sentences, with a staccato effect, interspersed by long Sanskrit compounds. However, in these novellas the style is simple with no high-flown Sanskrit. The first novella, *Ha Ha Hu Hu: A Horse-Headed God in Trafalgar Square*, reads well, with every sentence carefully constructed, though there are occasional lapses in syntax and in marking paragraphs, which could be due to irresponsible printing. However, by 1960, when he was writing *Vishnu Sharma Learns English*, Satyanarayana had grown somewhat carefree. He began writing novels by the dozen, often dictating several novels the same day to scribes who worked in shifts. He dictated sentences as he pleased, never looking back to read what his scribe had written. The manuscripts were sent to press as they were. No one edited his work, and apparently no one proofread it either. One can find paragraphs that run to pages on end, because the scribe was not told to begin a new paragraph.

The punctuation is inconsistent and spelling arbitrary. We do not have adequate information about the scribes themselves and their writing habits; and we have no way of checking if the spelling is the author's or the scribe's.

I call these novels oral novels, which have to be read with a different poetics in mind than those we apply to written novels. I tried to develop for my translation strategies that reflect the specific nature of the original novels. However, a certain degree of written quality inevitably enters my translation—for the very reason that I am writing and not dictating.

During the first decades of the twentieth century, the question of the dialect in which literature was to be written was hotly debated. Telugu literature until that time was mostly in verse. Classical metres were largely syllabic and they allowed only a fixed set of syllabic clusters to be used in a verse. Variations in the canonical shape of morphemes were not allowed in these metres. It was due largely to the continued use of these metres that the spelling of words and patterns of syntax in literary use remained fairly homogeneous through a period of about nine hundred years—quite a phenomenon in the history of any language. Furthermore, Sanskrit, which ceased to be a spoken language but continued to be used as a vibrant literary language for about a thousand years more, gave the Telugu literary dialect a source of sustenance and inspiration to remain uniform and distinct from its various spoken dialects.

However, the emergence of the printing press in the nineteenth century generated an increased need for prose.

Paravastu Cinnaya Suri (1809–1862), a Telugu scholar in the employment of the East India Company, wrote a grammar of Telugu modelled after the prescriptive style of the venerated Sanskrit grammars, efficiently encompassing the literary Telugu that had been in use for writing verses for about a thousand years. He thought his grammar could be followed for writing prose for discursive purposes, ignoring hundreds of years of the practice of using a different variety of prose in commentaries and common business transactions. The administrators of the East India Company, in charge of public education, most of whom were trained in England in classical languages, prescribed Suri's grammar in schools. However, the variations in syntax and in the spelling of words between what was acceptable in writing according to Suri's grammar and the way educated people wrote in their daily use was so great that they almost looked like two different languages. Young men and women were told that the words and sentences as they had habitually written them were ungrammatical, and they had to learn a whole new set of rules to learn how to write.

Modern scholar Gidugu Ramamurti (1863–1940), spearheaded a movement to change the way of writing Telugu. He called the language that followed Suri's grammar *grāndhika-bhāsha*, book-language, and argued in favour of adopting for writing *vyāvahārika bhāsha*, language used by educated people in their daily life.

His argument made a lot of sense: It was clearly artificial to try to write prose for modern use following the rules that were prescribed for writing verses in the past. However, when Ramamurti rejected Suri's grammar as outdated, it sounded like a call for rejection of grammar as such, like telling people they can write the way they speak—without any regulations. The Telugu literary community was divided into two camps: the 'traditionalists' insisted that Suri's grammar should be respected, and the 'modernists' argued that such restrictions fettered the freedom of writing. The arguments were fierce and the battles were endless. It was unfortunate that the debate lacked conceptual clarity. Gidugu Ramamurti, with all his great scholarship, failed to state that he was calling for a new set of regulations and conventions for a new *written* language, and not for a state of chaos where people wrote as they spoke. His argument in favour of a language used by educated people in their daily use (*sishṭa vyāvahārika*), left room for a lot of misunderstanding. In the confusion that followed, it was not realized that nowhere in the world do people write as they speak and that all languages develop written forms that change in time, but still remain distinctly different from speech.

Satyanarayana took the side of the traditionalists, primarily because most of his writing was poetry. But oddly, he continued to support the traditionalists even when he wrote novels on themes of contemporary life. However, as he began to dictate his novels, his style inevitably showed the influence of spoken forms. In the end, the style in which his later novels appeared came out in an incongruous mix of styles, old and new, with words written in a variety of spellings, neither following the old grammars nor following the contemporary spoken forms. His syntax, however, was brilliantly conversational and his sentences powerfully expressive. His desire to follow an outdated grammar failed to suppress his creative energy. In the end, what Satyanarayana achieved was an arresting atmosphere created by an entirely new language that could only be named after him. His prose style became the hallmark of his novels.

Dictating the novels caused other problems as well. As Satyanarayana dictated, he tended to digress frequently from the context of the narrative. Often the digressions were so far removed that whatever he was thinking at the moment found place in the novel, either as a part of the conversation between characters or as a long commentary by the author on the situation at hand. His novels acquired a charm of their own because of these digressions and are loved by his admirers.

While translating *Ha Ha Hu Hu* where such digressions were few, I followed the original fairly closely. But in translating *Vishnu Sharma Learns English*, I decided to take some liberties. To translate the printed text as it is might be of interest to critics who might wish to study the author's mind at work in dictation, but it would tax a non-Telugu reader, and for that matter, even a Telugu reader. Apart from the digressions, which impede the narrative, incidents with local and contemporary references would require endless footnotes. I abridged the novella, eliminated digressions and paraphrased some sentences rather than translate every word. I am aware that in the process my translation might change an oral novel into a written novel. But I hope the oral nature of the novel is still apparent. I made sure that the changes I made are minimal and do not affect the integrity of the story. I maintained the basic style of the narrative and meticulously preserved the dream.

On the Use of Diacritics

Diacritics used in this book are the general standard for transliterating Sanskrit, except that short ĕ, and ŏ, which are specific for Telugu are marked. No diacritics are used for names of people and places. Diacritics are used for titles of books and foreign-language words. The name of the author Viswanadha Satyanarayana appears in its popular English spelling, but when it is part of the title of a book, the spelling with diacritics Viśvanātha Satyanārayaṇa is used.

HA HA HU HU
A HORSE-HEADED GOD IN
TRAFALGAR SQUARE

One

One morning in London a number of people were gathered in Trafalgar Square. They were looking at a strange animal. It had the head of a horse; the rest of the body was human. It had a mane and its ears were erect. Its teeth, which were half visible, were flat and large, like grinding stones. It had a strange vertical mark on its forehead.[1] The body of the animal was like that of any human being: two hands, two feet. It wore anklets, but it was hard to tell whether they were made of gold or brass; they were yellow in colour, and looked more like bracelets. The animal wore toe rings with precious stones, armbands, shoulder ornaments, diamond rings on each of the ten fingers, wristbands embossed with lion heads and a crown on its head.

It was not clear whether this animal was dead or just sleeping—it was lying on its side. They were not even sure whether it was an animal or a human being. It had a silk cloth wrapped around the lower part of its body. An upper cloth, a kind of a shawl, with wide, golden embroidery lay torn at a distance. On its back, between its shoulders, there were two long, vertical wounds. A great deal of blood must have flowed from them. Some blood, clotted, was on the ground. The silk upper cloth lying at a distance was also stained with blood. It was summer but the nights in London were still cool and this probably helped stop the flow of blood.

The animal was tall; if upright, it might stand about eight feet high. Its chest was two arms wide.

People were looking at it from a distance. As the day advanced more people gathered and they began to talk.

There was a scholar of Greek among them. He said, 'The Greek hero Theseus killed an animal with the face of a bull, the Minotaur. This animal is something like that.'

A hunter, who had a great deal of experience with animals in Africa and South America and had captured some of them for the London Zoo, commented, 'I heard once about an animal in Africa with a horse's head and a human body. But I didn't believe it then. If only I had captured this animal. I would have donated it to the London Zoo. That would have gotten me the peerage. Now it's too late.'

Seeing the animal lying still, some children tried to get closer, but their mothers pulled them back.

'If this is really an animal, how come it has clothes? And jewellery?' wondered some people.

Others asked, 'If it's not an animal, what could it be?'

'This surely is an animal,' another remarked. 'An American or a Frenchman captured this animal in an

African jungle or some such place. He was probably taking it home in an aeroplane. It must have fallen from the plane and died. When it fell down, its head cracked and that's why it was bleeding.'

'If that were so, why does the animal have clothes? What is this piece of cloth tied around its loins and another for its shoulders! What kind of clothes are these? People wear slacks and jackets; who wears pieces of cloth?'

Another man said, 'I've heard that's what people in India wear.'

Then another voice was heard saying, 'Oh, I know, this must be some Indian's pet.'

'The people in India themselves are animals. Why would they need an animal for a pet?' snapped a man who looked very English. Everyone laughed.

Another man said, 'Indians never hunt in the forests of South America or Africa. Their government never lets them go. How could they get an animal of this kind and have it for a pet?'

'But then why does this animal have clothes that are like a Hindu's?' A smart person provided an answer to this question. The hunter who captured this animal probably lived in India for some time, and for the fun of it, he dressed his pet like a Hindu. Everyone thought that was smart thinking. Some were afraid that the animal might be awakened by the noise and asked everyone to be quiet.

'But then how come this animal has expensive jewellery?' asked another person. Nobody heard him. It was very noisy.

Some people said that the animal was dead and others said it was alive but only sleeping. Everyone feared that the animal might wake up and harm them, but no one was willing to leave.

The traffic on the streets stood still. More and more people gathered. The news spread all over London. High-ranking dukes, the Lord Mayor, the Archbishop—all of them came. Scotland Yard let them through. As a precautionary measure, the Lord Mayor had police officers surround the animal and stand some twenty yards from it with guns ready to shoot.[2] Then he and a few other important people walked close to it, with cocked pistols. The police drove away the people who had gathered around. Earlier, the people had gotten much closer to the animal without any guns. But the police acted officially, because that was how the police should act. While all the important people watched, ready with pistols in their hands, a clerk bent over and examined the animal. Word was sent to famous doctors so they could find out whether the animal was dead or alive. Heavy iron chains were brought and the animal's hands and feet were shackled. Now the animal wouldn't be able to do anything even if it should wake up.

The doctors came and examined it. They examined both sides of the animal for two hours and declared: 'It's not dead but we cannot say it's alive either. There's no breath. The heart isn't beating but seems to be sound otherwise. There's no pulse but the blood is still warm. The physical nature of this animal does not seem to conform to our medical knowledge. The body of this animal is very different from the bodies of animals we know. It doesn't look like any animal that exists on earth,' they declared.

The doctors' decision spread from mouth to mouth. People laughed at this. A zoologist who had brought a number of strange animals from Africa to the London Zoo, Mr Dickinson by name, ridiculed the doctors. If he had been given the chance, he would have figured out in a minute what type of animal it was.

The doctors examined the animal all over and couldn't determine what caused the two large wounds between its shoulders. However, one thing they were certain of, that it fell from an aeroplane. It must have happened sometime during the night. The animal probably tried to grab on to something behind it and that was how the shoulder blades were wounded. But then, if the animal really fell from such a height, shouldn't it have more wounds on its body?

They removed all the jewellery from its body, made a list of all the items and gave them to the police for safekeeping. The doctors applied some medication and dressed its wounds. All the while the animal lay still, without moving. They examined the cloth covering its body. It was a very fine piece of fabric. No one knew where such fine material was made. They had heard of Dhaka muslin, but they were not sure if it was as delicate as this cloth. In addition, it had an embroidered gold border. The beauty of the border was beyond words; it was light rose in colour, like the sky at sunset.

A hundred people lifted the animal into a big van. But where should it be taken? The zookeeper said the animal belonged to him, but the Mayor said that nothing could be decided until the nature of the animal was known, once it was awake.

So they built a big iron cage, thirty feet long, thirty feet wide and fifteen feet high, in front of Scotland Yard. A hundred policemen stood watch with loaded pistols in their hands. Ten doctors sat around the animal. By this time, it was dark.

What would the animal eat if it woke up? They brought horse gram, hay, bread and liquor. Everybody waited for the animal to wake up.

Two

For about fifteen days the animal did not move; then one day it started moving. On every one of those days, people had come in large numbers from all over Europe to see the animal. The hotels in London were all full; the city was crowded with visitors.

'It moved, it moved,' the news spread in a split second all over London. The soldiers stood in attention with loaded guns around the iron cage.

The wounds on the animal's back had not healed even after the doctors had bandaged them. It woke up. It spread its arms and legs, stretched, moved to the other side, and opened its eyes.

The police stood attentively.

The animal looked around. It looked surprised. It sat up, then jumped up and stood. It yelled loudly, '*Kim gadomhi.*'[3]

The sound was like the neighing of a horse. But for the people who were a few hundred yards away, it sounded like words, syllables. Was it a language? And if it was, what language was it? How could an animal speak anyway? Those who were at a distance and thought they recognized syllables were a little surprised.

By then it was noon. The animal looked at the iron cage and neighed. It sounded like laughter, but there was sadness in its eyes. It lay on the floor and made a sound as if it were in great pain. To those who were at a distance, it sounded like: '*Aho me athaṇṇatta im. Kim addi? Kim samadiṭṭho?*'[4]

The police thought that the horse was neighing in a strange way. A few older people in the group thought that there was more to learn about the animal.

A little while later the animal sat up and looked at the people. It did not look as surprised as before. The officers pushed the food closer to the animal. It looked at the food: bread, potatoes and horse gram. It didn't seem to know what they were. Then someone brought fruits and placed them before the animal. As soon as the animal saw the fruits it made a gesture that it recognized them. It picked up a fruit. The people thought that it would eat the fruit, but the animal examined it, turned it around and then put it back.

'The animal hasn't eaten anything for fifteen days. Why doesn't it eat that fruit?' someone wondered.

Some thought, for an animal of that size, that fruit was not enough.

'How could a horse eat fruit anyway,' said some others.

After a little while, the animal extended its hands through the cage and made a gesture, asking a person to draw near. Someone approached, and the animal neighed. To people at a distance, it sounded like, '*Koṇutumam*.'[5] People began to realize that the animal was trying to say something. But still the question persisted: 'How could an animal talk?'

The animal realized that this person did not understand what it said. It gestured with both hands to indicate pouring of water over the body. Nobody understood what it meant.

There was a Hindu in the crowd. He said, 'Maybe the animal wants to take a bath.'

The word slowly reached the Mayor. The Mayor thought that this might be true. But then, how to arrange for a bath for the animal? It would need a lot of water.

Some suggested that they should chain the animal's hands and feet and take it to the Thames.

'Oh no, that's very dangerous. It could kill people on the way,' said some others.

So they brought hoses from the fire engines and pumped water over the animal. The animal was all wet now. And it was muddy all around the cage. The animal took the cloth off its shoulders, wrung it out and dried most of its body. It wrapped the cloth around its loins and then pulled off the wet cloth it was wearing. Then it twisted that cloth and hung it on the iron bars to dry. The people were amazed at all this.

The animal gestured that the floor was all muddy and there was nowhere to sit down. People understood the gesture. They brought a big stool and handed it to the animal. The animal sat on the stool in the lotus position, closed its nostrils and began to meditate. Nobody understood what it was doing. After about an hour, it opened its eyes and stood up, tied the now dry cloth around its body and put the cloth it was wearing out to dry. It pointed towards the fruits, gesturing for more. The Lord Mayor sent his men and had a large basket of fruits brought in. The animal then gestured asking for a *chěmbu*.[6] Where could you find chěmbus in England! So they gave it a glass instead. The animal took the glass, sprinkled a few drops of water on the fruits, muttered something, waved its hand around the fruits and then ate all the fruits. It gestured for more water. They gave it more water from the hose. The animal drank the water.

Sitting on the stool, the animal looked quietly around at everybody. It laughed again. Now the people understood that that was how the animal laughed. The animal pointed towards the cage and gestured asking why it was there. Everyone was amazed.

Someone in the crowd said, 'No, this isn't an animal. This is a human being. The head is a horse's head but this surely is a human being. We have discovered new continents, but we haven't yet discovered the continent where people like this live. Let's find out what his language is and which country he comes from. Looks like he comes from a very civilized culture. Why put him in a cage? Get him out.'

The police officers didn't agree. 'We can't free him from the cage,' they said. 'How can we be sure that it's not an animal? What if it pounces on the crowd and eats people alive?'

So the cage stayed.

The officers talked about many things to the animal in English. It was clear the animal did not understand. Then they spoke in French, German, Italian and Russian, one after the other. Still the animal did not understand. They brought a black man and had him speak his language to the animal. Listening to all these languages, the animal began to laugh as if it were ridiculing them. The police didn't know what else to do. After a little while the animal neighed, which sounded to people at a distance like 'Kim ma e sudam? Kim edam?'[7] By now everyone knew that the animal was talking. But it did not know any of their languages, so they did not know how to communicate with it.

However, they noticed something interesting: The animal was totally calm and looked uninterested in the people around it.

All this time, the soldiers stood with loaded guns. Coming close to the bars, the animal looked at one of their guns. A soldier standing behind the animal was frightened and walked four paces back and held the gun close to him. The animal turned around and saw his frightened face. It realized that the man's hands held some kind of an instrument for killing. It looked at the gun with some interest and asked the policeman to see the gun. The policeman refused.

Everyone looked on in amazement.

The sun was setting. People were leaving for their homes. For fun, the eight-year-old son of a police inspector poked at the animal from behind with his badminton racket. The animal turned around as the boy ran away and stretched its hands through the bars to catch him. The boy escaped but the animal did get hold of a soldier, pulling the gun from his hands into the cage. People were frightened and ran away. Even the police and the soldiers were fleeing when the Lord Mayor commanded them to stop.

The animal began to look closely at the gun.

Three

The officers started wondering how to retrieve the gun from the animal. While they discussed several plans, the animal began to turn the gun around to examine it. Everyone was nervous; any moment its hands could touch the trigger and the gun could go off. If it were not for the command of the Mayor, the soldiers would have run away.

A senior inspector thought of a plan. He ordered a stray dog to be brought there and shot it while the animal was watching. The dog died. He then had all the police aim their guns at the animal and gestured to the animal to throw out the gun. Inside the cage, the animal looked closely at the gun, then saw that the inspector who had killed the dog was reloading his gun. We don't know what it thought, but the animal gave the gun back to the policeman. As it was giving the gun back, the animal must have pushed the policeman with the butt of the gun, because he fell on his back as he took it.

The animal began meditating all night with eyes closed. The police had given the animal two blankets. All these days the blankets were lying in the cage, untouched. Now the animal covered its body with one of them.

Meanwhile the zookeeper who had insisted the animal go to the zoo, sent an application to the Mayor and went and spoke to all the officials concerned. But the Mayor did not want to give up the animal. As a result, a rift grew between the zookeeper and the Mayor. The zookeeper then plotted to get the animal into the zoo while everyone was asleep. He made all the arrangements for that night, having bribed the police on duty.

Despite all this, he was rather afraid. Things like this did not happen in London. The Mayor was all-powerful. The zookeeper might even lose his job. But he still wanted to do it. People were that crazy about animals in that country.

That night while everyone was asleep, twenty people came in a truck and stood near the cage. The animal woke up from the noise, yawned and neighed loudly. All the soldiers woke up too. The zoo director realized that he could not carry out his plan and giving some excuse for his presence there at that hour, coolly drove the truck away.

Next morning the animal gestured that it wanted to take a bath again. As the police turned on the hoses, the animal gestured that it did not want to bathe that way. But then how else could it take a bath?

The animal made a loud noise as if it were trying to say something to them. To people at a distance it sounded like, 'Pucchassam, addhivā ettha ṇadī?'[8]

No one understood what it meant. The Mayor happened to be standing at a distance where he could hear that noise as words. It was a language and not animal sounds. He was astounded. All these days he had been too close to the animal and the sounds had been too loud to hear clearly. What language could this be? This was not an animal. This was a human being from some unknown country. However, history and geography tell us that there are no such human beings anywhere in the world. The Mayor stood there, at a distance, in case the animal spoke again.

It did. *'Pucchassam, addhivā ettha ṇadī?'*[9] The Mayor heard it clearly.

It was late morning. More and more people came to see the animal. Among them was a Sanskrit scholar, a professor from the University of London, an Englishman.

For two weeks the Sanskrit professor had been hearing about the discovery of a strange animal, but did not believe it. Scholars do not believe such things as easily as ordinary folk. He also heard that the animal woke up and that it was talking. He finally decided to go and take a look. He came and stood in the same place where the Mayor stood. He too heard the words the animal uttered.

'This isn't Sanskrit, but it sounds similar to it,' he remarked to the Mayor. 'There are many languages that came from Sanskrit, like Paisaci, a Prakrit language, and others. This must be one of those languages. I have a dictionary of Prakrit languages. I'll refer to it. Also, if the animal knows Prakrit, it probably knows some Sanskrit as well.'

The Sanskrit professor went up close to the cage and gesturing with his hand, said, *'Kim attha.'*[10]

The animal listened. Its eyes opened wide and its ears stood erect. It neighed loudly, stretching its hands wide. The scholar did not understand what the animal was saying. He repeated what he had said before again and again. The animal was saying something. The scholar didn't have a clue. After a while, he realized that the sound was just too loud for him to understand. Its throat was big and so it spoke in a loud voice, which sounded like a lot of noise. So the Sanskrit professor went and stood at a distance. This time he heard it clearly: *'Atra samīpe asti vā kascinnadī, snātumicchāmi.'*[11]

The professor went and told the Mayor, 'He wants to take a bath and wants to know if there is a river nearby.'

The Mayor's heart sank. How could they take the animal to the river? How could they give it a bath? If they let the animal into the river, it might not return to the shore. All the authorities sat and thought about it. Their first question was whether to give the animal a bath or not. And the next question was how. Setting aside the question of 'how' for later, they wondered whether they should take the animal to the river.

One of them said, 'What's wrong with giving it a bath? It looks like an animal from a hot country.'

Another person intervened, 'Don't say "animal". It is speaking Sanskrit. Sanskrit, they say, is a great language, and there are many great books in that language. How can someone who speaks Sanskrit be an animal?'

Still another said, 'It's all very confusing. We can't decide whether it's an animal or a human being. Based on its head, it looks like an animal. But from its language, it's a human being. His Sanskrit indicates that he comes from a great culture, and surely the clothes and jewellery show that he's civilized. I think we can let the animal take a bath.'

'How do you know that it's Sanskrit the animal speaks?' a police inspector demanded. 'The professor may have imagined it was Sanskrit. Moreover, how can you determine one's goodness based on language? One could speak a civilized language and still be a brute at heart. If you take this animal to the river, it might kill people on the way. Who knows? It could be like a hippopotamus. Once it's in the river, it might disappear under water. Later it might hurt us because we imprisoned it. We shouldn't take it to the river.'

Everybody was convinced by his argument. Also, if it was really a kind of hippopotamus, they thought they should not let it go without learning more about it.

'That would be a great loss.' they decided. 'We have collected so much knowledge about unknown continents like Africa, Australia and South America, and have written many books about those places. We shouldn't lose this animal without first studying it.'

The animal might get angry if they told the truth. They would say there is no river nearby. They had the message communicated to the animal through the Sanskrit professor. The animal listened, and it looked very sad. It was late in the morning, so they gave the animal a bath with the hose. After the bath, the animal meditated for a little while. They brought a basket of fruits and the animal ate them all.

Four

The news spread all over Europe: the animal could talk; its language was Sanskrit; it did not eat unless it had bathed; it meditated before meals. There was excitement all over Europe. A trainload of Sanskrit scholars from Germany arrived in London. A large facility was built, big enough for crowds to view the animal. The place was located on high ground and was very well-ventilated. The building had no walls; instead, there were iron bars. Surrounding the building was a vast open space and a high compound wall. They wheeled the animal from the cage into this facility.

This facility contained all the comforts the animal would need. There was a large cot made comfortable with two or three layers of cotton bedrolls and pillows in one of the rooms; attached to the room was a bathroom with a large showerhead, bars of soap and towels. On the front porch were several chairs—a couple of easy chairs and some ordinary chairs—all of them were huge, in proportion to the size of the animal. There was a storeroom too, with many varieties of fruit. The animal could eat fruit whenever it was hungry. They also realized that the animal needed a chĕmbu to drink water, so they obtained a few chĕmbus. They also had two suits specially tailored to its size. These arrangements took two months to be completed.

People began to go in and out of its new cage. About a hundred excellent Sanskrit scholars from Germany and France always stayed with the animal. They talked to it, recorded their conversations with it and published them in the newspapers of their countries. To reduce the loudness of its voice, they attached a gadget to its mouth. It toned down the sound and broadcast what it said so they could hear the words clearly. The scholars persuaded the animal to use the gadget and it agreed to wear it close to its mouth.

But then they learnt that human voices were too low for the animal, so they spoke into loudspeakers. At first the animal could not follow the European pronunciation of Sanskrit. Their /a/ was more like /e/, /śa/ was more like /sha/ and /la/ was closer to /ḷa/. They lengthened short vowels and shortened long vowels, so instead of 'nārāyaṇah' they said 'narāyanah'. Slowly the animal accepted it as a kind of Prakrit and got used to it.

An entrance fee was collected for seeing the animal. Viewing hours were also established. A smaller fee was charged for seeing the animal from a distance and a larger amount charged if one wanted to view it up close. If one wanted to talk with the animal, one had to pay ten pounds. Fees netted about a hundred pounds a day.

Some people noticed that the animal never slept. It ate only once in the morning after its bath and lay on its bed as if it were sleeping. Some of its activities were bizarre. It stood on its head for several hours a day; sometimes it sat with its legs folded, left heel tucked under its bottom, with the right heel on top of the left and held its breath. It did this for several hours. No one could talk to it during those hours.

The conversations scholars had with the animal were published in the newspapers.

People were eager to read about him. All over Europe newspapers published pictures of the 'horse-man', wrote strange stories about him and reported the conversations the scholars had with him. Here are some of them.

SANSKRIT SCHOLAR: Where do you come from? (*From now on, for the convenience of the readers, the Sanskrit conversations are given in translation.*)

HORSE-MAN: I don't know.

SANSKRIT SCHOLAR: Who are you?

HORSE-MAN: I don't know.

SANSKRIT SCHOLAR: How did you come here?

HORSE-MAN: I am not able to say anything about it. There is something vague in my mind, but I can't recollect anything.

SANSKRIT SCHOLAR: What is your name?

HORSE-MAN: Ah, wait a minute. Ha— Ha— no, I can't seem to remember.

SANSKRIT SCHOLAR: How did you learn Sanskrit?

HORSE-MAN: How did I learn? I don't know. I just speak it, that's all.

SANSKRIT SCHOLAR: Does everybody in your country speak Sanskrit?

HORSE-MAN: Yes, I think so. But I cannot recollect what my country is.

SANSKRIT SCHOLAR: What is your nationality?

The horse-man thought for a while, but did not answer.

SANSKRIT SCHOLAR: Have you heard of London in your country?

A German scholar asked if the horse-man had heard of Berlin and a French scholar asked if it had heard of Paris.

Then, suddenly, a Sanskrit scholar said, 'Your name is Hā Hā Hū Hū, is it not?'

The horse-man opened its mouth in surprise, and with wide-open eyes stood up, stretched its body, but suddenly looked as if it was in grief. A loud expression, *'Attha kim,'*[12] came from its mouth, like deep thunder. (It didn't have its gadget on.)

From then on, the scholars called it Ha Ha Hu Hu. It was too long; they shortened it, calling it Ha Hu. Everyone wondered how the Sanskrit scholar had known its name. The scholar had looked in a book of Sanskrit noun conjugations published in India. There, he found a word, glossed as 'the name of a gandharva'. He thought that 'gandharva' was a person from a race of people. He did not research further, but mentioned this to other researchers, who thought for a while and rejected the idea. Since the Sanskrit book stated that a gandharva was a class of people born from devas, gods, they thought that gandharvas must be people lower in rank than devas. But since they did not believe that devas existed in the first place, they rejected the possibility of this creature being a gandharva. However, Ha Hu's appearance and language conformed to what was said about gandharvas in Sanskrit books.

A select group of scholars held a secret meeting. They discussed whether it would be right to let people know that Ha Hu was a gandharva, one of the several races Hindus believe to be gods. They decided that revealing this might create problems. Soon the government got wind of it. With the Archbishop of Canterbury presiding, all the scholars took an oath to keep the secret from going beyond their lips.

Their intention was to give themselves time to thoroughly investigate whether this creature Ha Hu was really a gandharva. What if it wasn't a gandharva? Loose talk might encourage irrational beliefs. Scholars were ordered to research the matter. There was only one strong reason for saying that Ha Hu was not a gandharva. Gandharvas have wings and fly in the sky. It did not have wings. Moreover, gandharvas are beautiful; the horse-man was not. Therefore, it was resolved that it was not a gandharva. In any event, gandharvas did not exist.

Five

There was this great linguist in Germany; he did not believe that a horse could speak. A zoologist in France did not believe it either. How could they? Both of them were great scientists.

The linguist strongly believed that the human organs of speech were created in a particular way to make the sounds human beings make: dentals, palatals and such. He said to a colleague, 'Listen, if a person has thick lips or a thick tongue, or if the muscles of his mouth are too large, his pronunciation will be unclear. If the size of these organs is any bigger, he won't even be able to talk. That's why animals can't utter the sounds we do. Also, there's a certain flexibility to the human throat. Animal throats can only make harsh sounds; they aren't capable of producing syllables. The newspapers say that the sounds this horse makes are like language only when heard from a distance. Up close, it's like a big noise. It's probably just noise; they must be imagining that they hear a language.'

'But then,' said the colleague, 'the newspapers publish entire interviews with the animal. What about that?'

'The whole thing is fiction,' concluded the linguist.

The French zoologist did not believe the news stories either. He had examined the brains of many animals and had not found cells in animal brains that are similar to human brains. They are entirely different things: the human brain and the animal brain. It is not possible for a human brain to exist in an animal skull.

'I've examined the brains of a number of monkeys as well,' he said to his colleague. 'Their brains are a bit closer to human brains than other animals. They're supple. It is not possible to put such an intelligent brain inside the skull of a horse. The space is not big enough. You can see for yourself. The human head has a skull this big. There's a lot of space inside it. A horse's head doesn't have such a skull.

'In addition, there's a considerable difference between the head of a human being and that of an animal. A human head can grow hair. The ability to grow hair is inherent to the human head; it's partly a quality of the brain. Animals do not have hair on their heads. Horses and lions have manes, but that's not like human hair. The mane grows on their neck. Whichever way you look at it, it is impossible to believe these rumours.'

The linguist from Germany and the zoologist from France left for London. The linguist reached London first. He spoke with the Sanskrit scholars. A number of those scholars were also linguists. They agreed with what he said. The sounds of a language cannot be produced without what they call in Sanskrit 'inner effort' and 'outer effort'. There are stops, fricatives, nasals and a whole variety of other sounds. All this requires human intelligence. What Ha Ha Hu Hu has is only a horse's head. There must be further investigation, they agreed.

LINGUIST: You spoke with the animal—The Sanskrit scholars insisted that Ha Hu not be called an animal. He was a human being—okay, with *him*, for a long time. Did you talk to him from a distance or up close? And if you did get close, have you ever noticed the animal's—sorry, *his*—teeth or his tongue? How are they shaped?

SANSKRIT SCHOLARS: We haven't noticed. The sound he made was too loud to hear the syllables clearly. We had to attach a gadget to his mouth to reduce the volume. He speaks into the gadget so we never have the chance to observe his teeth or his tongue.

LINGUIST: Haven't you ever looked into his mouth, not even when he was yawning?

SANSKRIT SCHOLARS: No, we haven't. He did yawn a couple of times but he was standing up at the time. He is eight feet tall and we were not able to see into his mouth even when we lifted our heads.

LINGUIST: This whole thing looks like a fraud. It's possible that humans could grow eight feet tall. Such things are not unknown. Maybe the fellow put a mechanical horse's head over his own. Did you ever take a close look?

SANSKRIT SCHOLARS: No, we didn't. Everybody said he might hurt us if we got too close. Even though we were not ourselves afraid, we didn't go near him.

LINGUIST: Has he ever hurt anybody?

SANSKRIT SCHOLARS: No, never.

LINGUIST: Have you ever gone into his cage and sat near him?

SANSKRIT SCHOLARS: Yes, many times. He has never done anything to harm us.

LINGUIST: So, he is gentle, we have nothing to fear. We'll go see him. We'll ask him to open his mouth and we'll examine it ourselves.

SANSKRIT SCHOLARS: No, we shouldn't do that. It's not courteous.

LINGUIST: Strange. You're talking as if he is a gentleman. Moreover, this is a matter of science. You should convince him. Every intelligent person must make an effort to find out the truth in a scientific way. If he really has the teeth and cheeks of a horse and can speak like a human being, we would be able to teach all animals to speak like human beings.

SANSKRIT SCHOLARS: We agree. We believe that this is scientific research and we are after the truth. But he should believe this too, shouldn't he? If we are to examine his mouth, we have to ask him to lie down and open his mouth for us. He might consider it disrespectful. We've had a recent experience with him.

ONE OF THE SANSKRIT SCHOLARS: I took something from his hand without asking. He looked angrily at me, indicating that it wasn't proper. Do you think such a person would open his mouth for us?

LINGUIST: Well then, we'll have to put him to sleep with chloroform. Then we can examine him freely.

SANSKRIT SCHOLARS: It's doubtful that our drugs would have any effect on his body. He has two vertical wounds on his back, under his shoulder blades. They put medicine on the wounds during the first two weeks before he regained consciousness, but they didn't heal. The wounds are still there. He eats fruit, but we don't know why; he never goes to the toilet. During those first days when he was lying in the square, doctors examined him. There was no heartbeat or pulse. How can you force him to take chloroform? He has to let you reach his nose. We don't think he'll consent, but you can ask him if you want to.

LINGUIST: If, as you say, he's such a well-mannered and knowledgeable person, he will certainly consent to our request. But I don't know his language. So please translate my words to him. I have a feeling he'll agree. This *is* science, search for truth.

Together, they went to see Ha Hu. He was sitting, holding his breath. A scholar told the linguist that the way he sat was called *padmāsana* (lotus position) and that the way he held his breath was called *prāṇāyāma* (breath control). Ha Hu himself had told the scholars all this. A month ago, Ha Hu had meditated for three to four hours a day; now he was going for about seven to eight.

The next morning the French zoologist arrived and met with the linguist. They agreed it is impossible for an animal brain to work like a human brain.

The linguist said, 'In order to make certain human sounds a person needs to breathe from the navel and only humans can control their breath in the exact proportion needed to produce palatals, dentals, retroflexes and other such sounds. The human brain has the inherent knowledge required to perform all this, without our conscious effort.'

'Sanskrit grammarians also knew this,' said one of the scholars. 'They named these sounds *spṛṣṭa* (stops), *īṣatspṛṣṭa* (fricatives), *samvāda* (closed sounds), *vivāda* (open sounds), and so on.'

LINGUIST: Whatever they called these sounds, only humans are capable of making them.

ZOOLOGIST: Does the Sanskrit language have names for all these sounds? It must be a very civilized language, and those who wrote books on the grammar of that language must be great scientists.

SANSKRIT SCHOLAR: Compared to them, we are insignificant.

LINGUIST: Well, let's not worry about comparisons. But the unconscious efforts we make to produce these sounds—

SANSKRIT SCHOLAR: The 'bāhya' and 'ābhyantara' efforts—

ZOOLOGIST: Leave your technical terms aside. Those sounds cannot be produced unless there's human intelligence. The animal brain doesn't have that kind of intelligence.

LINGUIST: Your science and my science differ in methods but agree in the truth we find.

ZOOLOGIST: Human blood and animal blood are different from each other.

SANSKRIT SCHOLAR: That doesn't apply in the case of Mr Ha Hu. He has a human body. His body is even more delicate and softer than any human body. If the two of you still want to discuss the organs of speech and the qualities of the brain, you may do so.

LINGUIST: It looks like you're getting upset. We're only discussing science. We aren't being disrespectful to your horse-man.

SANSKRIT SCHOLAR: Sir, let's be clear about one thing. Ha Hu *is* speaking. That he speaks Sanskrit, we know. We have never read such beautiful Sanskrit in any book. He must be a great scholar. Since he speaks so well, it is obvious that the organs of his mouth are suitable to speech and that he has a brain comparable to the human brain. This is something you can infer from common sense. We don't see the need for all these invasive tests you suggest.

LINGUIST: We did not say that we would look for the obvious. We want to see if his speech organs are different from humans while still being able to make human sounds.

ZOOLOGIST: That is my interest, too. I want to see if his brain is similar to the human brain.

SANSKRIT SCHOLAR: How can you see that?

ZOOLOGIST: We have to put him to sleep and open his skull.

SANSKRIT SCHOLAR: You want to open his skull? You probably cannot put him to sleep in the first place. And what if he should die? If he stays here in our country for a little longer, we might find out where he came from, and who he is. We believe that he will reveal some great things. What we should be interested in is his knowledge and its depth. It is ridiculous to spend time on questions about his

organs and limbs. His knowledge appears to be superior
to human knowledge. There is no doubt that his brain is
different from a human brain. His throat is, of course, big.
You have seen it. It is as big as a horse's throat. There is
also no doubt that his cheeks and his tongue are big too,
or you wouldn't hear such loud sounds when he talks. I
don't think that one needs to cut his body open to see these
things.

LINGUIST: We seem to disagree on fundamentals. You
want everything to be learnt from imagination. We insist
on experiments. Your imagination won't lead to the truth,
but our observation from empirical data always leads to the
truth.

SANSKRIT SCHOLAR: We don't imagine something
from nothing. Our imagination is based on cause. If the
basis of our imagination is wrong, then our conclusions
will be wrong. Tell us if our basis is wrong. You could be
wrong too. You always want to collect facts. You might
miss some of them, and then your analysis would lead to
incorrect conclusions.

The linguist and the zoologist left, saying that they
disagreed on fundamentals. The Sanskrit scholar went to
see Ha Hu. The linguist and the zoologist talked to each
other and agreed that the animal must be put to sleep. Then
the zoologist could cut open his skull and examine the
brain, while the linguist would examine the mouth organs.
They would have to find a way to administer chloroform
to Ha Hu. They decided to do it without the animal's
knowledge. They feared that the scholar might report their

conversation to Ha Hu, but then they thought he wouldn't dare do such a thing.

The linguist and the zoologist wanted to take a look at the facility where the animal was housed. For three days and nights they monitored the animal's every activity. They noticed that the animal lay down to sleep at about midnight; this would be the most convenient time for their task.

Things continued as usual. People came to see the horseman; scholars talked to him. The linguist and the zoologist also came and looked around. They appeared to be planning something.

For nearly two weeks nothing happened. Then one night, around midnight, a group of about fifty people approached Ha Hu's cage without making any noise. They were very tense. One of them opened the door. A few days before, they had put oil in the keyhole so it would not make any noise. Six of them went in. They locked the door behind them. The rest of the people stood outside the cage with guns aimed at the animal. The six who entered and approached the animal also had pistols in their hands. At that time, Ha Hu's hands lay close to his belly and his legs were straight. In a split second, two men slipped heavy chains around his hands and feet. Not even a man with the strength of twenty-five men could break these chains.

As soon as he felt the chains on his hands and feet, Ha Hu opened his eyes. Immediately, ten electric lights were focused on his face. Lying still, Ha Hu looked at all of them. There was a flood of light all over the room. Ha Hu saw a Sanskrit scholar amongst the people around him.

The scholar yelled into his ears, 'We put chains on your hands and feet. If you move, we'll kill you. To help scientific research, we are giving you a drug to sleep. For about two hours you will be unconscious. Your life is not in danger. If you don't resist, you'll save both yourself and us a lot of trouble.'

Soon two doctors came close to Ha Hu and started administering chloroform. Ha Hu looked at all of them. Seeing the Mayor standing by his side, Ha Hu realized that this was going on with the consent of the government. He closed his eyes. The doctors began to pump the chloroform. One of them was reading Ha Hu's pulse. After about a quarter of an hour, they checked to see if he was conscious. Ha Hu opened his eyes. They continued for another quarter of an hour, and checked again. Ha Hu opened his eyes again. This procedure went on for an hour. Ha Hu was still conscious.

The linguist wondered if the animal was holding his breath. He removed the chloroform tube from his nose and checked his breathing. No sign of breath. The doctors examined his heart. It was not beating. They checked his pulse. Nothing. They feared that the animal was dead. They wanted to give him artificial respiration. As they were becoming agitated, Ha Hu opened his eyes. Everyone was amazed. The doctors checked his heart and pulse again. Still there was nothing. And yet Ha Hu was looking at them with eyes wide open.

Six

The Mayor and the two doctors removed the chains from Ha Hu's hands and feet, and all of them left. The police, who stood outside with guns, also departed. The linguist and the zoologist sat together with two doctors to plan their strategy. The French zoologist had lost all hope, but the German linguist didn't want to give up.

LINGUIST: What would have happened if we had cut his head open while he was awake?

DOCTOR: That would have been dangerous. The man would have died.

ZOOLOGIST: You think he's human?

DOCTOR: I really don't know. I've read some Greek mythology, even some Hindu mythology. Animals like this one appear in those stories, but I thought that it was only myth. In Greek mythology, the Minotaur and other such animals had life; Greek heroes killed them. Why would anyone kill them if they weren't alive? Life is indicated by a heartbeat and pulse, but in this man everything is contradictory. His heart doesn't beat, and he has no pulse, and yet he's alive; his eyes move. I really don't know what to think.

ZOOLOGIST: Maybe we should go to him and tell him about our scientific research, and convince him that there will be no danger to his life and that he will regain consciousness in an hour. Then he will probably consent to our study.[13] If he does not consent, there's another thing we can do. We'll show him a gun and tell him we'll shoot him. If we kill an animal right in front of him with the gun, he'll be scared. I think he'd cooperate with us then.

DOCTOR: Well, both suggestions sound fine. We'll go and talk to Ha Hu tomorrow.

Everyone left.

The next morning the doctors, the linguist and the zoologist went to see Ha Hu. He was doing his breathing exercises. They were surprised that he started so early in the morning. He did not open his eyes until evening. They waited and waited and then left.

They came the next morning. Ha Hu was still meditating. They asked the guards if he had slept that night. The guards said that he had not; he was sitting there the whole night.

Two weeks went by. Then one day someone saw that something like bird feathers were growing on his back. The wounds which had been on Ha Hu's shoulder blades were no longer there. Where had the feathers come from? Everyone was amazed. During the last fifteen days, no one had gone near him; no one had entered his cage.

On the sixteenth day, he opened his eyes and yelled, '*Tatra bhavantah kutra vartante?*'[14]

Hearing him speak, a policeman went and told the Mayor. The Mayor called for the Sanskrit scholars, who came.

Ha Hu asked for two large shawls. The shawls were brought. Soft, delicate, woollen shawls, three yards wide and seven yards long, with stitched borders.

He covered himself with one of them and said to the scholars, 'I want to take a bath. When I bathe, no one should be around. Or have something built here to give me privacy.'

The Mayor agreed to this request. This Ha Hu is really a civilized man, or he would not ask for a private bathroom, the Mayor thought.

They brought the required materials and enclosed the bathroom on all four sides.

Ha Hu went in, took his bath, came out and asked for fruit. They gave him fruit and he ate. Hordes of people came to see him. Scholars began to talk to him. Ha Hu always kept his shawl wrapped around his shoulders.

Several days passed. Ha Hu talked during the day but did not sleep during the night. He sat and did prāṇāyāma. The French zoologist and the German linguist thought that he stayed awake because of their recent attempts to put him to sleep.

When another week had passed, it became evident that under Ha Hu's shawl something was growing on his back. People thought it was the folds of the shawl, but whatever it was, it was growing even bigger. When Ha Hu sat, it looked as if golden feathers were spread under him. He went and took a bath before anyone else was up, and he sat still on the porch until sunset. Previously, he ate fruit; now he didn't eat any. Soon after sunset he moved a little and sat in the lotus position and resumed his prāṇāyāma exercises.

One day, in the afternoon, the linguist and the zoologist came in with two doctors and two Sanskrit scholars. They sat at a short distance from Ha Hu. Ha Hu reached for his second shawl and covered himself up fully. Only his face was visible.

The scholars told him in Sanskrit the intentions of the linguist. 'Sir, this gentleman comes from Germany. He is a professor of linguistics,' they began.

'What is linguistics?' asked Ha Hu.

One of the scholars replied, 'Linguistics is the science which studies how languages were born and which language came from which.'

Ha Hu smiled and said, '*Sarveṣām bhāṣāṇām girvānyeva prabhava hetuh. Yeṣā vicāraṇā nāma kim prakārā?*'[15]

SANSKRIT SCHOLAR: First, there were the Indo-European languages. From those came the Indo-Iranian language. Sanskrit came from the Indo-Iranian language. This is the conclusion of linguistics.

HA HU SMILED AGAIN: 'What else?'

SANSKRIT SCHOLAR: This other gentleman has come from France. He is a zoologist. Both of them are experts in their fields. They have a few questions to ask you.

HA HU: *Ka yeṣa kathyatām.*[16]

SANSKRIT SCHOLAR: Kindly excuse our curiosity. Your body is a human body and your head is a horse's head. Horses are animals. They neither have human knowledge nor the physical facility to utter human sounds. Since your head is a horse's head, the zoologist wonders how it is possible that a brain capable of human intelligence is located in it. Since your cheeks, teeth and other parts of your mouth are like those of a horse, the linguist wonders how you are able to make human sounds. In order to find answers to these questions, the scientists want to give you a drug to make you unconscious. Then they will cut open your brain and examine it. This experiment is to find the truth. Therefore, we request that you consent to it.

HA HU: What if I don't consent?

LINGUIST: We'll have to force you to consent. (The Sanskrit scholar translated this into Sanskrit for Ha Hu.)

HA HU: I wonder how your minds are capable of such thoughts. If I wanted to examine your brains to see why you have such thoughts, what should I do?

One of the Sanskrit scholars translated these sentences for the German linguist and the French zoologist. They looked at each other; they did not know what to say, so they merely sat for a while and then left.

A Sanskrit scholar said to Ha Hu, 'In our country there's a great thirst for knowledge. Our people go to other countries and write about all the strange aspects of their cultures.'

HA HU: What's the use of doing that? Don't you know that creation differs from place to place? There are many different animals on this earth. If there are many types of animals, their habits vary. If there are many types of people, their habits vary too. If one sees a new animal or a new human being for the first time, that might be a cause of wonder, but that's the product of ignorance. If, as a result of knowledge, the mind matures, there's nothing to wonder about. Furthermore, if you observe one thing, you can infer many things from it. Whatever we infer will not cause surprise, not even if you happen to see it in reality. Why do you people want to research everything? It doesn't look as if you focus your minds to find the truth of things. How much can you know through mechanical means? If you see with a totally focused mind you will find answers.

The scholars did not understand what he was talking about, but they went and repeated his words to everybody outside. The next day Ha Hu's words were published in the newspapers. Philosophers in Europe who read them began to wonder about the intellectual quality of the horse-man and many of them wanted to see him. Scholars and scientists did not know how to argue with Ha Hu; he refuted whatever they said in one or two words. People in London began to consider Ha Hu not as an animal but as a strange polemicist.

Seven

The linguist and the zoologist began to think about what they should do.

ZOOLOGIST: It doesn't look like we can control this animal.

LINGUIST: I think we should resort to our first strategy. We'll take a gun and kill a buffalo or a bull in its presence. We'll then point the gun at it and frighten it. That is the only way we can gain control over this animal.

ZOOLOGIST: Let's go and talk to the Mayor.

They went and talked with the Mayor.

'We already tried that,' said the Mayor. 'When Ha Hu first arrived, he grabbed a gun from a soldier. We shot a dog in front of him to show him that guns kill. He returned the gun to us. Clearly, he knows that living beings die if they're shot with a gun.'

ZOOLOGIST: So he is afraid of guns! Well, what are we waiting for?

The doctors, the zoologist and the linguist went to Ha Hu and told him, 'If you do not accept our request, we'll use force. We must conduct this research. We're not even concerned with our own lives in our search for the truth. A French scientist who was determined to find out if a person would die from an overdose of chloroform took an overdose himself and died. Many great scientists have killed themselves in the quest for knowledge. You must cooperate with us in this experiment.'

HA HU: So! A number of scientists died. What benefit was it to humanity? Based on what I have heard from your scholars, there is still a lot of ignorance in this country. Many diseases don't even have a cure. People still die of cholera, of small pox. People don't even live to be a hundred years old. Nobody ever does *tapas*.[17] Knowledge comes through tapas, not by cutting up animal bodies.

ZOOLOGIST: We haven't come here to argue with you. If you don't listen and do as we ask you to do, we'll have to shoot you with a gun and then conduct our research on your dead body. So think about it.

HA HU: I've heard that everyone in your country is a free citizen, that's what a scholar told me the other day. Is that freedom limited only to those who are born in your country? If a person comes here from another country, doesn't he have such freedom? I'm an individual. I have my own freedom. I don't give permission for my body to be used in your research.

The scientists bent their heads in silence.

The zoologist answered, 'Freedom is only for human beings, not for animals. You're an animal, so freedom does not apply to you.'

Ha Hu: All of us are animals. There is a difference in knowledge between human beings and other animals. Human beings are more intelligent than other beings. The difference is determined not by their form but by their intelligence. I'm as intelligent as you are. Therefore, you should treat me as you treat yourself.

Zoologist: No. It's not intelligence alone. It's also the form.

Ha Hu: Well, then, how do you know that your kind of form carries intelligence, and mine doesn't? I was born with this form and with this kind of intelligence. Based on your previous experience, these two traits did not occur together. Now they occur in me. Why don't you accept that I am different? Why should I alone be considered an animal? Every one of us is an animal. All living beings are animals.

Zoologist: We're stronger. You came to our country, so you must obey our commands.

Ha Hu: Where did I come from? How did I come here? If only you can answer these two questions, I will surrender myself to you.

They decided that it was futile to argue with Ha Hu, so they gestured to each other that they should leave. Ha Hu's cage was locked behind them. The soldiers were given the command to shoot at Ha Hu's arms and legs. The bullet went through his left arm. It made holes in the shawl that covered his body. Ha Hu sat still. He did not even appear to feel pain. The soldier shot another round at him. This time the bullet hit his right arm. Ten shots were fired.

Every place a bullet hit, it made a hole in the shawl. Bullets went through his body but he did not move. Just once he appeared to be in pain. The soldiers stopped firing. Ha Hu moved his feet a little, sat in the lotus position, and began his prāṇāyāma

Five minutes later the soldiers fired again. This time, the bullets bounced off his body, fell to the floor and started a fire. Ha Hu sat in the middle of the fire. After twenty rounds, the soldiers went in to see what had happened to him. They put out the fire that was burning around him and looked at him. The shawl that covered his body was all burnt up. From his back were hanging large, long golden feathers. He looked angrily at the soldiers. They ran away.

Ha Hu closed his eyes again and sat quietly for a moment. When he opened his eyes he asked for four more shawls.

The linguist and the zoologist said, 'Let's give him the blankets only if he agrees to our request to examine him.'

The Mayor and the Sanskrit scholars said, 'No, that would be wrong.' They gave him the shawls.

The doctor said, 'He might consent to our request in a few days. Let's wait.'

The police began to talk agitatedly amongst themselves. 'When we first fired at Ha Hu, our bullets hit him, but he did not seem to have been hurt much. Later, he was totally unscathed by the bullets. They fell off of him. We're lucky he didn't kill us. If he had turned on us, we would be dead by now.'

The soldiers were afraid to be near Ha Hu.

One of them said, 'He's a good man. He doesn't do us any harm. If he wanted to harm us, he'd have done so a long time ago. We don't need to be afraid.'

They were probably scared, but they had to obey orders. They knew their guns were of no use, but still they held them and stood guard.

A week or ten days later, the treachery that was committed against Ha Hu faded from memory. Sanskrit scholars began to go to see him again. One day the linguist and the zoologist also went to see him. Ha Hu noticed them and smiled at them. A shiver ran through their bodies.

Ha Hu looked at the scholars and said, 'Listen, these two men thought that I was an animal. In fact, I'm a human being, an animal and also a bird.'

He stood up and took off his shawl. There were two huge wings between his shoulders. He flapped his wings. People fell down as if they had been hit by a typhoon. As the two wings moved briskly, the iron rods of the cage broke in several places. A brilliant golden light filled the room. People's eyes were dazzled. Everyone stepped back in awe. Ha Hu took a few paces; it sounded like horse's hooves hitting rocky ground. His body were shining as if it were made of gold. He looked as if he were about to fly. When he stood up, with his wings spread out, his eight-foot body looked as tall as a palm tree, like a mountain with wings. Overwhelmed by the vision, some of the people closed their eyes; some fell flat on the ground; some were shivering; and a few even fainted.

Ha Hu closed his wings, covered himself with his shawl, and returned to where he had been sitting. Seeing that the people around him were frightened, he gestured to them to come to him, assuring them that there was nothing to fear. He took the broken bars of the cage, set them aside and sat in the open. Many people came near him.

He looked at the Sanskrit scholars and said, 'Human beings, animals, birds—all of them have different natures on this earth. But in another place, in a place you do not know about, it's possible that the features of an animal and a human being and a bird could exist together in one living being. Our body takes its shape in accordance with our intentions.'

No one understood what he was saying. What does he mean by our bodies taking shape according to our intentions? A couple of the scholars happened to have read books by Max Muller. They seemed to have understood something of what Ha Hu said.

The sun set and everyone left. Ha Hu spent the night in the open, without bars, without a cage.

Eight

The papers published the news that the horse-man now had wings, that they were strong and the bars of the cage broke when he flapped them. People in America, Europe, Australia, Canada and Africa, who had earlier been amazed that he was impervious to bullets, now made a bee-line for London. Almost everyone who had money to spend was on his way to London.

The Mayor, the senior officials of the city and members of the Parliament gathered to discuss the situation. Everyone said that since the horse-man was not harmful to anyone, it was not proper to imprison him. It was decided that one of the Lords should take him as a house guest, or he should be taken as a state guest and given residence in the Parliament House.

The next morning the senior city officials and the scholars went to see Ha Hu. They read him a proclamation:

O human being, who is neither an animal nor a bird!
You are a good person. You have as much knowledge as

48

any human being. You are not cruel. We did not know that before so we imprisoned you. Since we now believe that you are harmless, we release you from prison and take you as a guest of our country. The State provides you with all the facilities and comforts you need. Now that the State has given you protection, no one can do you any harm.

When the scholars explained in Sanskrit to Ha Hu the contents of this proclamation, he laughed aloud and said, '*Aho alpatā manuṣyāṇām.*'[18]

The scholars didn't translate Ha Hu's words. Ha Hu was then taken to the residence of a prominent Lord, where he was provided with royal comforts.

People began to argue.

'What are those wings for? Does he fly? Where does he fly to? Maybe they should have kept him in prison. What if he flies away in the middle of the night? If he flies away during the day, aeroplanes could chase him. Releasing him was a bad idea,' said one person.

'But how do we imprison him? When he hit the iron bars of his cage with his wings, the bars broke. When the police shot at him, the bullets failed to hurt him. He is staying here because he likes it here. There's no way of forcing him to stay,' said another.

Yet another person said, 'These wings and the horse's head all seem to be fake. They aren't real. If the wings are real, why were they not there in the beginning? How did he get them now?'

When he went to the Lord's house, Ha Hu asked for a big room for himself and that no one disturb him for a month. The Lord informed the officials of the state. They thought at length and accepted his request. They decided that he would probably sit meditating, as he had done before. They provided all the facilities that Ha Hu would need in one large room. Ha Hu went into his room.

A month passed.

On the thirty-first day, the Lord went and knocked on the door. Ha Hu opened the door, but the Lord did not see anyone in the room. The Lord was afraid that Ha Hu had disappeared. Ha Hu realized this and said, 'I'm here behind the curtain.' It looked as if there was a curtain.

Things returned to normal. Scholars and other people came to see Ha Hu.

One day the Archbishop and ten other bishops came to see Ha Hu. They asked him about his religion.

HA HU: I have no religion. What do you mean by religion?

BISHOP: You shouldn't say that. Religion is what you call in your language, *matam*. There is God. Jesus is the Son of God. We should believe in him. He is our Saviour. That's our matam. What's yours?

Ha Hu looked at them strangely. He closed his eyes and went into meditation. The Bishops tried to wake him up with a million questions. He did not answer.

After a while, Ha Hu said, 'Ordinary people do not have any matam. Only sages have matam. People believe what the sages say. Small people have small beliefs. Great people have great beliefs. Everywhere, either in this country or in another, all living beings are blemished by desires. He who contemplates the Eternal, is free from desires, is not affected by any problems. Why do we need a matam? All that we need to know is the impermanence of this world.'

Nobody spoke after that.

Late one afternoon the Lord took Ha Hu out for a drive. Ha Hu sat in a big car. The Sanskrit scholars sat around him. It was still daylight. The car went slowly. They drove along the Thames River. Ha Hu looked at the steamers, the great city of London, its large streets and the statues set up in the squares. He saw the entire civilization visible in the city. When he saw the river, he asked that the car be stopped.

He looked at the scholars and said, 'You *have* a river here. Why did you say there was no river nearby?'

The scholars said that they had not known about it.

A large crowd gathered to see Ha Hu. By that time, it was evening. Ha Hu and his party returned home.

Early the next morning, the Lord, Ha Hu's host, went to see Ha Hu. He was not in his room. Soon there was a telephone call from the police. Ha Hu was taking a bath in the Thames. London was still sleeping. In less than half an hour, all the people who had been sleeping were at the river. There was a traffic jam. People were everywhere, on the ships, even on the masts of the ships.

Ha Hu was taking a bath. When he went under water and shook his wings, he made huge waves like those in an ocean during a storm. Even the big steamers that were anchored at the dock rocked and tilted to their side. Small boats capsized. Ha Hu went under water and then jumped up and shook his wings. Water from the waves flowed through his wings in big currents. People on distant ships were drenched from the water sprayed from his wings. When he went into the river like a big whale, water flowed around him and it looked as if the river split into two streams. When he hit the surface of the water, it sounded like a thunderbolt. He was like a big elephant in a small pond and the Thames overflowed. His bath created major problems for the people in the vicinity. Nobody knew how to get him out of the river.

After about an hour, he came out. It was still cold in the city. He walked towards the house of the Lord where he was staying. The scholars and the Lord himself walked behind him. Ha Hu went and sat in his room, and began his prāṇāyāma. At twelve o'clock at night, he was still at it.

Early the next morning, he went to the Lord and woke him up. Some of the Sanskrit scholars went with him. Ha Hu said, 'Your river is small. When I was taking a bath in it this morning, a few boats capsized. I realize it is dangerous. Rest assured, I will not go to the river again.'

'That is exactly what we have wanted to request of you,' said one of the scholars.

It has been ten months since Ha Hu arrived. Stories of him have spread all over the world. Even people in India have come to know about him.

Some traditional scholars in India said, 'He must be a gandharva. He must be there due to a curse.'

Some others said, 'He isn't a gandharva. He must be some kind of spirit, a strange quirk in God's creation.'

Other smart fellows said, 'It's all a gimmick.'

Still others said, 'Why not? There are strange creatures. Haven't you heard of King Kong?' People from India, China and Japan went to see Ha Hu. People from every religion tried to find a parallel of him in their own mythology.

Nine

Sanskrit scholars began to talk with Ha Hu more often.

SANSKRIT SCHOLARS: It has been more than eleven months since you came to our country and we don't know anything about you. You haven't told us anything about your country either. What are your plans? Do you want to stay here? Or do you want to go and see other countries as well?

HA HU: I don't know yet. I'll be able to let you know in a few days, by one means or the other. I don't need to see any other countries. I can't tell you how much longer I'll stay here.

SANSKRIT SCHOLARS: If you go, where will you go?

HA HU: As I was saying, I'll let you know later.

SANSKRIT SCHOLARS: You know more than ordinary human beings know. Could you tell us about life after death?

HA HU: Why don't you ask your religious gurus?

SANSKRIT SCHOLARS: Our religious gurus answered this question in one way. Is their answer correct?

HA HU: Whatever the gurus of a particular religion say, is correct for the followers of that religion. Knowledge forms itself in accordance with the *samskāra* of the people. By your very nature your ability to believe is limited to what your gurus say. For example, a small fish lives in a small pond, and a big fish lives in a big pond. A whale lives in the ocean. If you put the small fish from the pond into the ocean, it will die. Our bodies are formed in accordance with our samskāras. And our mental capacities are formed in accordance with the environment in which we live, the body which we inhabit and the actions of our ancestors. This is an unbreakable bond.

SANSKRIT SCHOLARS: We know all these things. People have written many scientific works on these subjects.

HA HU: Then what is there for me to say?

SANSKRIT SCHOLARS: Tell us about life after death.

HA HU: Don't you have books on that subject in your language?

SANSKRIT SCHOLARS: Yes, we do; but we do not have a firm belief in them.

HA HU: That is what I've said. Belief varies with the person. It varies with his varṇa, with his jāti. If a person believes in one thing and you speak to him about another, he won't believe it. Suppose you talk about an ocean to a person who lives on a mountain. Suppose he believes it. What's the use? But let us say he went and saw an ocean. The quality of his belief has changed somewhat. Suppose he travels on it. The quality of his belief will change even more. Suppose he goes underneath the surface of the ocean and picks up gems. That is a totally different experience. But even then, does he know the totality of the ocean? Our beliefs are related to our experiences. Whatever we deeply experience, that is what is real to us. All other things are mere words. Therefore, it's much better to know a thing by experience than to gather information about it.

What Ha Hu said was published in newspapers all over Europe.

Eleven months after Ha Hu first appeared in London, the astonishment over his form had diminished. Everyone took it for granted. Among the scholars in Europe and America who read his words, some said he was a philosopher. Others said he was a prophet. Some considered him a thinker. More people wanted to see him. People came in large numbers, wondering how an animal could speak.

Ha Hu said, 'You printed my words in your newspapers, and when people read them, why did their idea that I am an animal grow stronger rather than weaker?'

One day a group fetched Ha Hu and showed him the railway, steamboats, machine guns, printing presses and telegraph machines. They explained to him in detail about each of them. He listened to them with interest.

SANSKRIT SCHOLARS: We have invented great things in this world. Other people have not discovered so many new things, but we have. Is it not amazing?

HA HU: There's nothing to be surprised about. If a certain mind acts in a certain way, thoughts related to that activity are generated. Then things like this take shape.

SANSKRIT SCHOLARS: No other nation has invented as many things as we have.

HA HU: Well, they did what they should. You know of India, don't you?

The scholars said that they did. Ha Hu did not speak any further.

From there, they took him to a zoo. The zoo was very large, like a large African forest.

'This is where you really belong,' said a scholar, teasing Ha Hu.

Everyone entered the zoo. When Ha Hu walked in, a couple of animals glanced at him. Suddenly all the animals in the zoo made loud noises simultaneously. The din was so loud that people were unable to stay there. Some large animals tried to break their cages and get out. A few monkeys, two elephants and three or four crocodiles escaped from their habitats. No one could imagine the reason for this agitation. Ha Hu listened to the animals and the ruckus they were making and took the scholars away from that place.

Four days after that incident, there was a big feast in the house of one of the Lords. Ha Hu was invited to the feast and he went. Scholars sat around him. It was exactly twelve months since Ha Hu had arrived in London. At eight o'clock in the evening, dinner was served. At eleven, the feast was over.

A famous German musician was going to play new music he had composed on the piano. Ha Hu had heard that there were great musicians in Europe, but he never had the opportunity to hear them. Now there was this

German musician. He was short and his face very red. He was dressed in black slacks and a white shirt. He sat near the piano and when he put his fingers on the keys, the keys produced waves of sound. He started singing in a deep voice as he played. Waves of sound were spread throughout the room, like horses neighing.

Ha Hu stood up and walked towards the piano. The scholars walked behind him. Ha Hu watched closely as the German musician played. Everyone was wondering why he was observing so carefully. People thought that he was attracted to the new sound. The German musician was making beautiful music. Music merged into the air, like sugar dissolves in water. Everyone was charmed. The German musician stood up and took a bow.

Soon Ha Hu sat down at the piano. He put his fingers on the keys and produced beautiful notes. People were amazed.

Ha Hu called a nearby scholar and gave him a closed envelope and said, 'Open this tomorrow.' The scholar took the envelope.

Ha Hu continued to play. He started singing in the *dhaivata*. The beauty of that note was new to the people. The German musician looked on in wonder. These were strange sounds, like water coming out of a full vessel with a small opening, like the waves of the ocean breaking on the flat rocks on the shore. Ha Hu sang for about half an hour. Nature stood still.

He stood up, looked around and left the piano. Now he was only singing. After a little while people looked at him and there was a stringed instrument in his hands. He was plucking the instrument with his fingernails. Everyone listened quietly. Their minds were totally engaged in the music. How did this instrument come into his hands? Nobody thought about it. All Nature was absorbed in the sense of hearing.

Soon Ha Hu was not there. His music was heard from the courtyard. People followed the music into the courtyard. Ha Hu was flying in the sky. He was playing the vina. The sound of his music was reaching the earth like waves on the ocean. The music was fading into the distance. Soon people realized that he was flying away. A few aeroplanes were ordered to chase him. Some returned; some did not.

The next morning, the scholar opened the envelope and read the note. This was the message Ha Hu had written in Sanskrit:

Animals are still close to Nature. That is why they made noises when they saw me in the zoo. Man is destroying himself by ruining Nature. Some time back a scholar asked me a question: 'What do you think of us humans?' This is my answer: I have not seen more ignorant beings anywhere else. I'll tell this to my people, the gandharvas.

VISHNU SHARMA
LEARNS ENGLISH

One

'I hear you're writing another novel. Is it finished?'

'No, it isn't. Writing a novel isn't that easy.'

'They say it's easy for you; you just dictate and somebody else does the writing.'

'It's true that I dictate, but I know it isn't easy.'

'I came to hear your novel. Will you read it to me?'

'It isn't done yet. What's the fun in listening to something unfinished?'

'What's it called? You always give your novels jazzy titles.'

'*Vishnu Sharma Learns English.*'

'Who is he?'

'Vishnu Sharma, the ancient author of *Niticandrika*.'

'How can he learn English? We don't know when he lived and back in those days English didn't even exist. You tend to write mythology.'

'Then don't listen to my novel. I didn't ask you to. You're the one who came here wanting to hear it. Now about the name of the novel, yes, Vishnu Sharma belongs to ancient times. But dead people are reborn, you know, and if they were born in this day and age, they'd have to learn English.'

'Where was he born? How old was he? What are the names of his parents? Which caste was he born into? Where did he go to school? There are so many questions,' he said.

'That's why I am writing this novel. He isn't really born again; he appears in my dream. That Tikkanna who wrote the Mahabharata, he comes too. He asks me to help him get a job. I don't have a job myself, though I have passed my MA, and know some English and Telugu, and even a little Hindi. I am like this fellow in the proverb: The doorway is hardly big enough for him to pass through, and he carries a drum around his neck. But he is Tikkanna, isn't he? So I try to get him a job, and I try to teach English to Vishnu Sharma. This has been killing me. I have no time to eat or sleep. People usually want to sleep. But I dread it. I don't really sleep; as soon as I doze off, the dream starts and I struggle. I become anxious; I want to get up, to be awake.'

'Come on! Your story doesn't make any sense. How can anyone think of waking up while he's asleep or while dreaming?'

'Why not? It has happened to me!'

'I don't want to argue with you. If you were born in another country, they would worship you; they would say there was no writer like you, your picture would hang on every wall in every house. But here, you swim against the flow of time.'

'Well, why shouldn't time follow me? I write the way I write. Do you want to hear it or not?'

'That's why I came, didn't I?'

'Before I begin the book, I have written a little something about dreams. Listen to it first. All people dream. Normally, each dream is a separate dream. That's not how it is for me.

'Every one of my dreams flows into another dream. There was this poet called Nidradaridra, "Deprived of Sleep". He only wrote a single verse in his entire lifetime. Once, he dreamt of a beautiful woman. He fell in love with her. For some reason or the other, she was upset with him. He wanted to go to sleep again, with the hope that he would dream of that girl one more time so he could make up with her. But he was so in love with her that he couldn't sleep, never able to dream of her again. So, he wrote a poem about her. But my story is just the opposite. I cannot stop dreaming the same dream. This is how it began.'

~

I was taking a nap in the afternoon. Two men appeared in my dream. One of them was light-skinned, kind of plump, with a little tummy; he had the Brahmin thread across his shoulder; it was somewhat soiled. He hadn't shaved and he wore a dhovati above his knees. The second man was taller and darker. He wore earrings and a tuft of hair was hanging from the top of his cleanly shaven head. He wore a dhovati with double-coloured borders. He had on gold bracelets

and a ring shaped like a grass-knot. He had a shawl on his
shoulders. His face was bright and intelligent.

I asked both of them to sit down. The first man sat
down, but the other did not. I wondered why. It could
be because I did not invite him properly, standing up and
showing him his seat. But I was sleeping, how could I get
up? And why was he so proud? Who was he anyway? One
can receive a person only when one knows who he is, right?
That is why we introduce ourselves with our clan, lineage
and given names saying, 'I, such and such, of such and such
a clan and lineage, greet you.' If you announce your lineage,
one can know who you are. But he didn't tell me anything.
Maybe he did not think I was worthy of his greeting. But
now he came to me, I didn't go to him, right? Forget the
greeting. Couldn't he just say: 'I came from such and such
a village, my name is so and so. I came to see you on such
and such business.' Furthermore, he didn't come from a
neighbouring town, nor have I met him before. He came
from heaven. You will know all about it when I tell you
the whole story. In any event, I got this irresistible desire
to laugh when I saw him: what a crazy man this is! But if I
laughed, I would wake up! So I didn't laugh. Then I asked
the man who was sitting: 'Who is this man, Sir?'

He said, 'I don't know. He looks like he has performed
a *yajña*. He must be a wealthy and important man, a
Somayāji.'[1]

I said, 'Who are you, and what can I do for you?'

'I will tell you in a minute, but take care of his business
first and send him off.'

But then the other man said, 'I am here on important business. It can't be finished off in a minute. Finish his business first.'

Now I thought that they were going to finish me before I could finish their work. What to do? I thought for a minute and asked the second man to sit. He kindly sat. Now both of them were seated all right. But they didn't tell what they came for. I can't sleep too long in the afternoon. I must get up by about 2.30 p.m. or 3.00 p.m.

So I said to them, 'Simple matters can be taken care of during the day, but if you need to stay long come at leisure during the night. I usually sleep at about 11.00 p.m., and won't wake up until 6.00 a.m. That's seven hours of time. Even if I should get up once or twice in the middle, I go back to sleep right away. So, please go now and come back at night.'

They didn't move. I thought I was done for.

I said, 'Sir, why don't you go?'

Both of them said, 'We can't. We didn't come here to go right back.'

My God, what a mess! My wife is not home. She went to visit her parents. I am getting by eating this and that. How can I feed these people? Moreover, they did not seem to be the restaurant types. They are going to sit right on my head demanding that I feed them. And I didn't have a cent on me.

I didn't know what to do. Suddenly I remembered that it was a Sunday. I didn't have to go to work. I took a deep breath and said, 'Sir, you can tell me later what you came here for, but first tell me who you are.'

Each one asked the other to go first, but no one did. It is like the two friends who were about to board a bus full of people. One or the other has to get on first, but each one says to the other, 'After you,' 'After you,' and the driver goes crazy.

I thought of pointing to the fat man myself, the man who sat squatting. He was no small figure. Maybe he had not performed a major sacrifice, since he did not wear earrings and lion bracelets, but he must be a scholar.

They say pandits in our country looked like him, simple, like common men. But, my goodness, you start talking to them and you will know each one is a scholar in six shastras and four Vedas. This Somayāji had performed a yajña but looked like a diplomat. This fat man, however, sounded naive. So I asked him, 'Swami, you tell me first. What did you come here for? What can I, an ordinary man, do for scholars like you? I am a humble Telugu teacher in a college. I will try to do the best I can to help you. But today is a Sunday, no offices are open.'

'If it's a Sunday, why should they close offices?'

I immediately knew these people belonged to a dead age. Who on earth would not know that Sunday is a holiday?

'Sunday is a holiday, you know,' I said.

'No, I don't. Why is it a holiday?'

'There is no school on Sundays so we don't teach on Sundays,' I said.

'What! You don't teach on Sundays! I can understand
if it is the eighth day of the moon, if it is the full moon day,
new moon day, or the first day of the moon. If you teach
on those days, learning does not flourish. You should never
study on the first day of the moon. That's why Valmiki
says about Sita emaciated in captivity: *"pratipat pāthaśilasya
vidyeva tanutām gatā."'*

I did not understand the meaning of the Sanskrit
phrase. Sure, I have an MA in Sanskrit, but if you ask me
why I did not understand this verse, well, we read Sanskrit
in English translation and wrote our examinations in
English. We don't know much of the Sanskrit roots and
suffixes. We don't quickly grasp Sanskrit in complete
sentences. I didn't even get that word pratipat. But then
I am a scholar, aren't I? Is it not a loss of face if I admit I
did not understand what was quoted? So, I kept proudly
silent.

'I don't understand why Sunday should be a holiday,'
he added.

I said, 'Sir, when God began to create, He started on
a Monday, went on for six days, He was exhausted, He
rested on Sunday. Since then Sundays have been holidays.'

The big fellow cracked up. The Somayāji was more
restrained. He got up from his seat and stood silently.

I was enraged, 'What do you think? Are you saying
there is no God, that he did not create this world?'

'No, I'm not saying that but how could God be tired?'

The Somayāji intervened, 'If man is tired, God could
be tired too. God is the cause and man is the effect. A

quality which is not in the cause will not be present in the effect. Therefore, we should agree, God *was* tired.'

'Fine, but how do you know that he rested only on a Sunday?' said the fat man.

The Somayāji did not respond.

If these people know so much logic, I know it too. Using some of my skill in logic I said, 'If God should rest one day or the other, why can't that day be Sunday?'

Both of them were floored by the power of my logic.

'Yes, you're right,' they agreed.

But the fat man would not stop. 'All right, if you want to, let Sunday be a holiday, but the full moon day, the new moon day, the first and the eighth days of the moon— declare them holidays, too.'

I don't make these rules, but I wanted to talk like one who does. Or else these people will kill me with their logic— cause and effect, existent and non-existent, on and on.

'No, we cannot do that,' I said. 'You say that if one studies on the first day of the moon, his learning does not flourish. Did I get you right? [I had understood from their conversation that pratipat means the first day of the moon. See, I am smart after all.]' I said this like a king who rules this whole country.

The fat man was taken aback. 'I don't know,' he said, 'that was what Valmiki wrote: Sita was emaciated like the learning of a man who studies on the first day of the moon.'

Now, I understood the meaning of the line from Valmiki he quoted before. 'Forget about all those things,' I said. 'For the last two or three hundred years in this country we have been studying on the first day of the moon. We are passing MA, doing doctorates, earning anywhere from two thousand rupees a month. What you say does not hold.'

I thought that he would be silenced but he was clever. 'Maybe all that you learn is not learning, that's why you get it,' he said in a snap.

My heart sank. I thought it was like losing your tongue while trying to heal your velum. What do I do? How do I protect my position of importance? They came to me; I did not go looking for them. I should have the upper hand.

Meanwhile, the Somayāji said, 'That was learning for those times, and this is learning for these times. You should not study for that knowledge on the eighth day of the moon, on the new moon day and so on, and for this new learning, you should not study on Sundays.'

My point won; I did not win. I must say something in order to emerge the winner. Therefore, I said, 'You took the words right out of my mouth. But there is something more. There is no prohibition that you cannot learn well if you study on Sundays. It is just a day of rest.'

And before finishing, I asked the fat man, 'What is your name, Sir?'

'I am Vishnu Sharma of the Bharadvaja clan,' he said.

The Somayāji perked up and said with great affection, 'I am a Bharadvaja, too. Let our clan flourish.' He waited a while and added, 'You don't seem to be a Telugu poet. Have you written in Sanskrit?'

'O, yes I did write in Sanskrit, but who cares. No one remembers me. I am the one who wrote the book called *Pancatantra* in Sanskrit. What did you write?'

'I wrote the Mahabharata in Telugu,' the Somayāji replied.

'Are you Nannayya?' I asked in excitement.

'No.'

'Sir, are you the great Tikkanna?' I asked.

He nodded in assent.

'Welcome. Please sit down, I cannot get up. If I do, I'll wake up, my dream will end and your business will be left undone.'

Tikkanna finally sat down.[2]

'Please tell me what you came here for,' I said. Then I suddenly remembered that I did not properly invite them, give them water to wash and sip. I had not said, 'My house was purified by their presence,' or anything like that. So, I said, 'Ayya! Come again at leisure. Now I am even unable to show you the honour of a proper reception. But wait, let me at least get you some water to wash your feet.'

I got up to get water and that woke me up. There was no Vishnu Sharma, no Tikkanna. I felt bad for waking up. Would they come again, or not?

They said they had some business with me. So, I thought they would come again. Next time I will be better prepared. I will store two vessels of water under my bed, so I can ask them to wash with it. I should give them something to eat. I can't get anything from a restaurant; they don't cook with good ghee. If my guests eat what the restaurant people cook, they will get sick. I spent the day thinking of them. Night fell.

Two

That night, as soon as I fell asleep, the two of them came and sat right in front of me. I was surprised.

'You came so soon!' I said.

'We never left, we stayed right here.'

'Here! Where? You've been here since the afternoon, aren't you hungry? I brought some food for you. It's under my bed. Please eat.'

'We won't need food yet for another four or five days. We get hungry from then on.'

'How so?' I asked.

'I came from heaven,' Vishnu Sharma began to explain. 'There is no hunger or thirst in heaven. Ever since I wrote the *Pancatantra*, my fame is spread all over the world. As a result, I went to heaven. I lived there all these years. Of late, there are many problems there. People from this human world die and come to heaven. None of them stays as long as we stay. They stay some four or five days. That is like four or five years in human time. They've done a

few good things during their time on earth, for which they
get to go to heaven for a few days. After the merit of their
good deeds is spent, they are sent to the place they deserve.
The noise they make during the few days of their time in
heaven is enormous. They behave as they please. I generally
stay away from them. But then a smart alec among them
raised a controversy about me. He said I didn't write the
Pancatantra. According to him, some unknown author
wrote it, and that person invented my name. This was his
proposition. I didn't pay any attention to him but he had
a lot of support among his fellow earthlings. All of them
wrote a petition, signed it and gave it to the king of heaven.
Indra laughed at it and dismissed them. But they refused
to leave; they all yelled that the issue must be investigated.
They have a right to stay in heaven for a few days; they
cannot be punished no matter what they do. So Indra
summoned me and asked, 'Tell me, Vishnu Sharma, have
you written the *Pancatantra*?'

'Yes, your majesty.'

'But these people say you did not.'

All of them turned to me and said, 'You are not Vishnu
Sharma. No, Vishnu Sharma does not look like you at all.
He wrote so many stories teaching success. How can such a
person be fat like you? He should be thin and full of energy,
with smartness written all over his face. Your face is dull.
We do not accept your claim to be Vishnu Sharma.

'I was mad. Not with them, but with Indra. People of
the age of decay come here and speak nonsense, but why
should Indra let them have their way? He is no atheist;

he is a Vedist. Why should he have to call me to defend myself? But what is the point in blaming Indra?

'When I looked at Indra, he said, "This is people's rule. If all of them say yes, it is yes; if they say no, the answer is no. There is nothing I can do. I am helpless myself. God Vishnu caused harm to the land by incarnating himself as the Buddha. Muslims and the English people came after him and fell like a hammer blow on a sore finger. Those English people, you know, they are lower than the lowest. Their education is what brought all this trouble. Let alone you, they are aiming at me. They deny the very existence of *svarga*, this heaven. They say svarga is not this luminous world in the sky. It is Tibet, which you know, is on earth. Trivistapa, the name we gave to our world, they say, is actually a cognate of Tibet. Trivistapa = Tibet? What happened to /sh/ and /p/? If the name of our land was Tivit, it can change to Tibet. I don't follow all this, it is confusing. The fuss they make in heaven is immense. In the old days when the anti-gods Ravana, Hiranyakasipu, Vritra and Naraka invaded, we fought battles with them and when they won, we ran and took shelter somewhere. There is no fighting of battles with these people; no swords, no spears. The only weapon these people use is pseudo-knowledge. We say that is a cow. They say it is not. Never mind their denying it, they deny that the Telugu word *āvu* is derived from the Sanskrit *go*. I am in deep trouble with these people. When they leave, others like them come in their place; there is no end to it. Anyway, why don't you show them the manuscript you wrote?"

'I said, "Where can I get that manuscript? It was written some thousands of years ago. Moreover, I didn't write it with my hand. I don't know how to write. We never counted writing as part of learning, you know. I dictated it, and some scribe wrote it. What evidence can I show that I was the author?"

'Indra said, "When did you write it? Do you know of any people who were around at that time? We will call them as witnesses if they happen to be in heaven."

'I thought for a while but could not think of anyone. After some time, I said, "I hear that a man called Cinnaya Suri translated a part of my book into Telugu and another person named Viresalingam translated the rest. Call them if they are here, they might speak in my favour."

'Indra thought for a minute and said, "I believe that Cinnaya Suri is here. Viresalingam left; for some reason he was angry with heaven."

'All those people who petitioned against me said in one voice that if Viresalingam should agree that I was the author of the *Pancatantra*, they would agree too.

'I said, "What is this business of someone else agreeing that I am Vishnu Sharma? Every one of you is someone, right? Aren't you you, unless someone attests you *are* you?"

'One of them said, "Yes, that is how it is."

'I asked why this was so.

'He explained: "Suppose you go to a bank to cash a cheque, someone who knows you should certify your identity, or you can't cash your cheque."

'I said, "But what if there is a man no one knows, what about him?"

"'Too bad, he can't be helped."

'I was amazed at this logic. I mastered five or six disciplines. I wrote the *Pancatantra* for the benefit of the world. That was my crime. I looked at that man who was talking to me and asked, "What is your name?"

"'Daniel," he said.

"'If I say you are not Daniel, what would you do?" I asked.

"'I have my birth certificate from the municipality records of my town," he said. "My school has a record of my date of birth and my high school diploma shows my name, my height, weight and notes my birthmarks. You can't deny I am me. It is no folklore. You show me what evidence you have to prove that you are you."

'I felt like I was half-dead. Man, O man, what do I do now? My date of birth was never recorded. I did not go to any school. No one recorded my birthmarks. I was at a total loss.

'I said to Indra, "Lord, Lord of the three worlds, I feel that your situation is worse than mine. I can't blame you. Even Rama had to send Sita off to the forest when a common washerman started talking about her. If you want me to go back to earth, I will obey, even though I am not anywhere comparable to Sita. I will go and see what I can do about my identification marks and all that."

'Meanwhile, someone brought Cinnaya Suri. Everyone said he was Cinnaya Suri. He looked quite dignified. He wore a coat buttoned up to his neck. He wore a turban and an *uttarīyam* on his shoulders.

'I asked him, "Sir, Are you Cinnaya Suri? Do you have any evidence that you are really him?"

'He said, "I worked in the schools run by the British government. I can bring four white masters to testify that I am Cinnaya Suri."

'"Very well," I said, "You translated two chapters of the *Pancatantra*—'Gaining Friends' and 'Separating Friends'— into Telugu, right? Can you tell me who wrote the book?"

'"Vishnu Sharma."

'I felt very relieved. But all those people cried in one voice, "No, no, we do not accept."

'"What to do now?"

'They all said, "Viresalingam should come and testify, that's the only way."

'I said, "All right, bring him in. I understand he left because he was angry with heaven. Please ask him to come as a favour to me."

'After a long while, Viresalingam came. An old man, he had a trimmed moustache, wore a red turban and a black coat. He came and stood but unlike Cinnaya Suri, he did not greet Indra. My heart grew heavy. Wishing to end this quickly, I asked, "Viresalingam, Sir, who wrote the *Pancatantra* in Sanskrit?"

'He replied, "We don't know who wrote it. The text has a very ancient history. Most probably the stories came from Greece and someone rewrote them in Sanskrit. We cannot even say they were written by one person. It is just like the Mahabharata which was not written by Vyasa but by many people who in the end gave the name of Vyasa. The *Pancatantra* is a similar case. Anyway, it is not much of a book. It was written for the entertainment of children."

'I said, "Why, then, did you translate it into Telugu if you didn't think much of the book?"

'"What Viresalingam wrote is not Telugu," Cinnaya Suri intervened. "It's a noise of clattering rocks. I translated the first chapter into an easy, delicious style. My second chapter is somewhat harder, but still the most beautiful Telugu. There are only two remarkable prose works in Telugu: one is the *Bhāratasāvitri* and the other is my *Nīticandrika*."

'The hundred or so people that were gathered there were furious. They yelled, "Do you dare insult Viresalingam? He is as great a writer in prose as Tikkanna is in verse. Hey, Cinnaya Suri, you might think you set the standards with your grammar. But you know, we tore your grammar to shreds. One of our men has cremated you already. You are not really alive. You are here because this is an old-fashioned heaven. You just wait. Soon our people will send a rocket into this heaven and conquer it. Then you will see what will happen to your Indra, your Nannayya and all the others."

'Viresalingam left regretting that he came to a place unfit for him.

'I said to Indra, "Lord, you cannot live with this crowd. I will go back to earth and get the education suitable for these days. Maybe I will write another book."

'What could Indra say? He said, "Fine." As I was about to leave, he stopped me with a wink of his eye. The crowd was slowly leaving, one after the other. When all of them had gone, Indra said to me discreetly, "Why do you worry about these people? They are not going to stay here; this is temporary riff-raff. I cannot say a word against them as long as they are here. I will teach them a thing or two later. Now, you want to go to earth? Well, if that thought came to your mind, you have got to go. You don't have to enter a mother's womb and suffer all that hell. There is this man on earth, go to him. He will take care of you. He will teach you English."

'I asked if this man knows Telugu and Sanskrit.

'"He thinks he does," said Indra. "All of their learning is like that these days. He is a little better among them, like a squinter among the blind. If you quote a verse in Sanskrit, he pretends to understand. If you go to any other person, he might say, 'Sanskrit is a dead language, if you keep on speaking Sanskrit, I will have you jailed.' So, go to this man. First, appear in his dream. I will make you free from hunger for a few days. It is difficult on earth to live free from the pangs of hunger. Learn English. Get a job and live on your own. But, listen, if you get bored, come right back. I will save your apartment in heaven for you. You must learn English. You will teach it to me when you come back. They say that even women in India know a lot of English words. That's *some* language! Someone told me God and dog are the same in that language; you invert dog and it becomes God! Anyway, I will let God Vishnu worry about it. You know, he took many avatars but never one as a dog."

'I said, "God Siva did that."

"'See, you are certainly fit to learn English. You are on the right track. Go. He sleeps in the afternoon. Go at that time and appear in his dream. He will do the rest."

'That's my story. You are my support, feed me milk or feed me water,' Vishnu Sharma concluded.

'We don't have milk and water separately. Our milk is always mixed with water. The farther your house is, the more water you get,' I said. Vishnu Sharma did not understand. He asked, 'What house?'

I explained: 'We have this milkmaid. She comes from Macavaram, about five miles from here. She has a couple of water buffaloes. Whether or not they give milk, she brings four containers of milk every day. On her route, she supplies milk to about two dozen houses. By the time she comes to my house, the four containers are still full. As she goes, she replaces milk with water. The farther she goes, the more the water. We still call it milk because it is white. Therefore, I won't feed you milk and water separately, I will feed them together. I will teach you English in the medium of Telugu. Do you know Telugu?'

'I am a Telugu man.'

I was elated. 'From now on, I will declare in my talks that Vishnu Sharma is a Telugu man,' I said with pride.

'What's a talk? Is it a discourse on a discipline? A refutation of the opponent to establish your position? What is it?' he asked.

I could not resist laughing. I laughed, but I did not wake up. I knew I would not wake up. You know why? Indra sent them into my dream and so he protects the dream.

'You don't know what a talk is? Discourses, disciplines, refutations, establishing—these are the words of the bygone days of BC,' I said.

'Who is Beecee? A great king of ages past?'

'BC stands for Before Christ. Your lesson begins right now. There was a man called Christ. We began counting years from him. It is nineteen hundred and sixty years since he was born. We believe only things that happened during this period as fact. Anything else is not trustworthy. If anyone says an unbelievable thing, we say it is a thing of BC. We use it also to mean that it is out of date, it does not work now. It's a new word for you. Write it down.'

'I can't write, you know,' he said.

'Sir, return immediately to heaven. Indra said you could come back, didn't he? These days, people who cannot write are considered illiterate idiots,' I said bluntly.

'What is this?' he said in honest amazement. 'So what if I can't write? I am a scholar. I can read, I just don't write that's all. Writing is what a scribe does. There are scholars and there are scribes.'

'Well, then we are all scribes here. Scholarship is optional. There is no need to be a scholar. There are a few people you might call scribes. They are not quite scribes, though. They are typists. We have typewriters. When an officer dictates, typists hit those typewriters. That's more a symbol of power than scholarship. Well, if you can read, it is not that bad. You can learn to write in no time.'

Vishnu Sharma said, 'But tell me about the talks you give.'

I said, 'Ayya, I am one of the great public speakers of this country. I get invited to give speeches.'

'What for?' he asked.

'Nothing. Speeches are for speeches. We have a number of colleges and high schools. They invite speakers to give inaugural addresses and valedictory addresses, and such. Every college has a Telugu association. They invite us to talk. We go and give talks.'

'What do you talk about?'

'Well, each of us has some favourite topics. I have a few. One is the greatness of the Telugu people, another is Vemanna's poetry and the third is the influence of English on Telugu literature. These are the topics I mainly speak on.'

'You always speak on these same topics? Won't the listeners get tired if they have to listen to the same things over and over again?' asked Vishnu Sharma.

I laughed and said, 'They never listen. They sit talking among themselves or laughing with each other. They pay no attention. They do their thing and I do mine. They listen to one thing, an obscene joke. To win their appreciation we talk about erotic things in the name of aesthetics. They listen to that with great interest, cooing and howling. When they don't listen to our speeches, what does it matter how many times we repeat the same speech?

I managed thirty years with these three topics. Can't I go on for ten more years?'

He said, 'All right, begin teaching me starting tomorrow.'

I had only one worry: for three more days they are taken care of. But after that, I have to feed them.

Three

Tikkanna, who was standing there listening to our conversation said, 'You consider Vemanna a poet?'[3]

I was taken aback. It's natural, I thought, that one major poet should feel jealous of another and said, 'Yes, not just a poet, a major poet. We think he is as great a poet as you are.'

Tikkanna grimaced.

'What's wrong?'

'I don't know, we never considered him a poet. He was a yogi; he wrote some verses. Anybody can write such verses.'

I intervened, 'Yes, you are right. Many of our modern poets are writing like Vemanna, and some now write better than he did. In fact, there are poets whose entire fame rests on such poems.'

Tikkanna continued, 'What's there in it? Is it poetry? Does it have an aesthetic effect? He wrote abusively of some traditions of Vedic life; he didn't quite understand them. If you don't understand you write like that but then, you can't call it a composition. If it is, even prose can be called poetry.'

I wasn't pleased but I kept my cool because of my respect for him.

'You don't think Vemanna is a poet? You know who said he was a poet? The same person who said you are a great poet. Did you know that?'

'What does it matter if he said it? People make mistakes.'

'No way, he is not the kind to make mistakes. You might be, but he is not. He wrote this thick book; we use it in our universities as a textbook. Vemanna is a very skilful writer. He can express profound thoughts in simple words. He criticizes society, condemns bad traditions, his writing flows with similes. He gained total control of the true Telugu idiom. He is a master of *āṭavĕladi*, you know, the metre named after dancing girls.'

'That's why he became a yogi. Get a dancing girl and you will be a yogi, too.'

'No, we banished all nautch girls from our country. Now we have singing girls instead, *pāṭavĕladis*.'

'Too bad, you have lost the chance of being yogis,' he said.

'Forget about yogis. You know what our people think nowadays? A yogi is selfish. He wants spiritual bliss for himself alone. That is wrong. All your traditional ideals are wrong. We rejected all of them. But coming to the point, you were so incensed when I said Vemanna is as great a poet as you. There is another person as great as either of you. If I mention his name, you will run away from here and will never want to look at the earth again. Vemanna at least wrote verses, be they simple in metre. But this third person never wrote a verse in any metre. We think he is superior to either of you. Recently, one of our critics wrote that there was no Telugu poetry before him, no real Telugu language. Our poetry, our language, begins with him. He is so great.'

I stopped, expecting that he will beg me to tell him his name. I wanted to make the announcement after a huge suspense, like the explosion of a cannon. But he wasn't the least interested. I continued to tease him, 'He has no titles like you have, Friend of the Poets of Both Camps, nobody called him Creator Deity of Poetry, as they called you, and neither did he perform a yajña rite like you did—nothing— you don't need any of these trappings to be a true poet. Hold your breath! I am going to tell you his name . . . here it comes . . .'

Tikkanna started laughing. My theatrics didn't bother him in the least, not even as much as the bite of an ant. But I was unwilling to retreat; I had come too far. I changed my tone somewhat and said: 'Ayya, Tikkanna, you might be fearless, you might be the creator-God of Telugu poetry; Errapragada might be your disciple; Nacana Somanna might have walked in your footsteps, someone else might have said your "literary creation is impossible for any other to repeat". All that might be true, but times have changed. Owing to the true principles of modern literary criticism we created, because of our knowledge of the evolution of language, because of the enlightening brilliance of the bright light of clear knowledge shining all over the world today, all of the old texts have been rendered worthless, values have been revolutionized; we decided that you three are poets of the same order—first, you, second, Vemanna and third, Gurajada Apparao.[4] Except for the needs of chronology, we would have put him first on the list.'

Tikkanna asked, 'Who is he? I have never heard of him. Is he alive or dead?'

'According to us on earth, he died.'

'But he did not come to heaven!' wondered Tikkanna.

'Why should he be so unlucky? Viresalingam might even have condescended to visit once. He was involved in performing marriages and whatnot; you see? He was a bit conventional. But Apparao doesn't even mention the name of your heaven. Why would he come there? Ayya, he is not the kind that would accept heaven. He is truly independent. He doesn't believe in the mythical lands that are known only from the second-hand reports of old texts. You know the land you call Kailasa, where God Siva lives, the one right at the top of the Himalayas. Our own Tenzing visited that peak recently. A couple of white men also went with him. We don't have to go that far back into history; recently, just recently, some Chinese men went up there and planted their flag. Until now, we used to think that climbing Kailasa was impossible for humans. But those people went up and returned in a breeze. Kailasa is now easy. If the great Kailasa has come within our reach, your heaven is nothing. Anyone could go there. Don't be too proud that you have an exclusive place unreachable to Apparao and his ilk. We don't need to send Apparao to plant our flag in heaven. Even greenhorns, poets who are still wet behind the ears, any of our junior poets could close the curtain on your heaven. We wanted to send some of them there, but all of our poets are chaste people, people of impeccable moral principles. They have conquered desire. They were disgusted when they heard that your heaven is full of whores, *chi*, a red-light district in heaven! Rambha, Tilottama, Urvasi, Ghrutaci—are they women of the sky? They are prostitutes, they have no morals. Our poets have decided never to visit such an immoral place. I cannot even list how many of our poets have written against heaven and its prostitute culture. So Tikkanna, don't expect that Apparao will ever come to heaven.'

I concluded my lecture. I learnt the skill of lecturing from Apparao himself, reading his books, that is. Apparao wrote that when Girisam went, I suppose, to Poona and gave a long lecture, all the professors in the town were stunned flat. I wanted to use that weapon against Tikkanna. But look at this sentence Apparao wrote: 'When Girisam gave a lecture for a full hour, non-stop, all the professors of the town were turned into *dung*!' Look, that turn of phrase, his Telugu idiom and the spoken rhythm of his sentence, which captures Telugu people's hearts. Show me anything close to this in the entire Bharata of Tikkanna. Can Tikkanna ever learn this skill? He must be born a thousand times before he can learn to write like this. This man who does not even accept Vemanna as a poet equal to him, will he ever learn to accept Apparao? If he comes back to our land, learns English, and sees how skilfully we combine English and Telugu in our daily use, then, maybe then, will Tikkanna realize that he wrote the Bharata in poor Telugu, and see the beauty of Apparao's style. It is not enough to boast, 'We wrote great books like the Mahabharata, and we live in heaven.' That doesn't settle anything. Who cares? Unfortunately, because we have nothing else to choose from, we select a few verses from his writing and teach them to kids in school. Those kids grow up and recite the same verses at public gatherings. His fame rests on that kind of popularity. 'Hey, Tikkanna, those days are gone, Vemanna got that status long before you. Today, it is neither Vemanna, nor you! Did you see that?' I said.

I was not all that comfortable talking in this vein to Tikkanna. But I was afraid he might end up staying as an uninvited guest. I just wanted to get rid of him.

No, it wasn't possible. He was more stubborn than I was. He said, 'I know what you're saying. I also know the changes you have undergone. Why did I come here then? Let me explain with an analogy. In the old days in our land, there used to be religious gurus who went on tour to visit their disciples. They went, gave them their blessings and received their gifts. That is all gone now. No one accepts them as gurus any more. The disciples have learnt English and are making good money, and so are the gurus. Yet, there is an occasional oddball that goes out on tour to visit his disciples. That's what I am doing. Sitting there in heaven, I thought about all this. Someone, I was told, had translated the Ramayana into English. He also translated the Mahabharata. However, the Mahabharata didn't get to be as popular as the Ramayana. I even felt like coming down here to learn English to translate the Mahabharata myself. Vyasa did not seem to be bothered by any of this. However, there are a few people here in the Telugu-speaking area that respect me as a poet. Even though they say I am a great poet, they do not know the deeper beauties of my text. I came to teach them how to read my books.'

'Listen,' he continued, 'we will go to a place of your choice. You will announce to the people that Tikkanna has come down from heaven and will talk on the Mahabharata. Collect an admission fee of one rupee. You will get a lot of money, at least in the beginning. Meanwhile, I will look for a job.'

I was curious and asked, 'What kind of job?'

'All the Telugu professors of the universities here are my disciples, right? I can go to any one of them and ask him to let me do his job for one year. I don't think they would refuse.'

This man must be crazy, I thought. He thinks that these are still the times of king Manumasiddhi and emperor Ganapati Deva.

Four

There is no way I can attend to them right now. First they must come into the human world. I can't do anything for them until then. Imagine it: I take Tikkanna to give a talk. I introduce him and say, 'Heeeere's Tikkanna,' but no one would see him. It would be like the story of the emperor's new clothes. Everyone would laugh at me.

So I told them, 'Look, here is the problem. Even I can only see you in a dream, how can others see you? Let us say Vishnu Sharma does not need to be seen by other people. I could teach him English in my dream. But then, if my family hears me talking in my sleep, they will think I am delirious. They will think I am dying. At the moment my wife is at her parents' house, but she will return in two or three days. She is a village woman. If I tell her, "You silly, I am just teaching a certain person English. He came to me in my dream and asked me to teach him," she will think I am insane. She has two brothers, strong as demons. They will pick me up and put me in the lunatic asylum. For your part, you will be safe; you will go back to heaven.'

Tikkanna said, 'Don't worry, the ethereal form we now have will last only three more days. From then on, we will look like ordinary people, like you. We will walk about like humans and everyone will see us.'

'That's fine then, but you should turn into men before my wife comes home. If you suddenly materialize as men in her presence, she might think you are ghosts, or thieves. She would scream out loud. Suppose I am at school at that time and the neighbours come with big sticks and beat you up. It would be of no use if you tell them, "I am Tikkanna." "Really?" they would say and would beat the *tikka* out of you. If there are any schoolkids in the group, they might recognize Vishnu Sharma by name. Some of them might have read parts of the *Nīticandrika* in their Telugu prose textbook. But you cannot count on it. These days, more and more textbooks use some other authors for prose selections. The *Nīticandrika* is not being used much. Even if it is used, the introduction is often left out. So they would not know that Vishnu Sharma wrote the *Nīticandrika*. If you tell them, "I am Vishnu Sharma," it would be like crying for help in the wilderness. No one would care. So, please get your human forms before my wife comes home. Today is Sunday. My wife will return on Wednesday morning. You should become men by Tuesday night,' I said.

'That's not possible,' Vishnu Sharma insisted. 'We cannot become human men until Thursday. Let your wife come on Wednesday. We won't talk to you that day. There need be no fears of delirium or insanity. We will see you Thursday morning. Meanwhile, tell your wife about us. Tell her two Brahmins will visit you, and they might stay for a few days.'

Tikkanna added, 'I might stay for a week or ten days, but Vishnu Sharma will be here for four or five months.'

'Do you think I can learn the language in four or five months?' asked Vishnu Sharma.

'Are you kidding?' I said, 'We begin learning English when we are seven or eight years old and go on learning until we are twenty-five. Even then we are not sure we have learnt the language fully. There is a joke among us: we begin with A, B, and it takes twenty-five years to get to read the letters from the other end—that is—BA. There is an examination, if you pass that, you get a degree called a BA. You won't get your high school diploma until you are fifteen. If you fail the exams on the way, you will be forty by the time you get your BA. How do you think you will learn all this in four or five months? You must be very greedy.'

'Any discipline can be completed in about six years. Why should this learning take fifteen years?'

'Longer than that. The BA is not the end of learning. There is another degree called the MA and then there is the PhD. What do you think this is, some kind of discipline in Sanskrit? The fellow is hardly twenty-five, and he says he has completed grammar to the last text, or he has mastered logic from beginning to end or that the other fellow is a scholar in four disciplines—logic, grammar, hermeneutics and theology. I get furious when I hear such things.

Thanks to the lords who rule us, we are able to claim we know English even though we don't know the language well enough and still assume our learning is superior to all the many disciplines the Sanskritists have mastered. That's the greatness of English learning; it has a beginning but no end. And you want to master it all in four months? Sure you do, you came from heaven!'

I thought that with this lecture Vishnu Sharma would be scared of English. I am in no mood to teach him. Apart from that there is another problem to be solved when my wife comes. She might not want to cook for them and feed them. She might protest that these people are a pain in the neck. Furthermore, when she has her period, I usually manage with my amateur cooking. Now I have to cook for two more people. Tikkanna cannot cook; you don't even have to ask him. Vishnu Sharma might cook, there's a possibility. People say, our old scholars gained all their learning with meagre resources. The author of *Gadādharīya*, that great book of logic, his name is Gadadhara—he is a Bengali—went to serve as a cook for a wedding feast. A few guests were discussing logic during the meal. They were arguing incorrectly, when this man who was serving them soup corrected them. They were amazed and asked him who he was. He said he was Gadadhara. His name was known all over the country from Kashmir to Kanyakumari. He was a great scholar but served as a cook to earn money. That was how they learnt then, for the sake of learning and not for earning positions. There is a good chance Vishnu Sharma knows how to cook.

So I asked Vishnu Sharma, 'Ayya, when my wife is having her period, could you give me a hand in the kitchen?'

'I can give you more than a hand. Don't worry on that account. I am a great cook. In addition, I will also teach your kids. After all, I taught the princes the entire discipline of "Success in Politics" in six months. I can do the same thing for your sons.'

I was scared stiff. I fell on his feet and begged, '*Baboy*, don't even think of doing that to my sons. Your success and our success are two very different things. Please don't make my sons scholars of the Sanskrit discipline of success. We have to do our studies in our own way for twenty years. No, we cannot finish it all in six months. Suppose we do that, it is like pouring rose water on ashes. It goes to waste. No one values it, no job, nothing. This rotten Sanskrit learning, what good is it? One should get a high school diploma, do a BA and all that gradually. If one says, "I learnt everything in six months," no one is going to give you a job. You have to live on begging. So, please don't harm my sons' future. I will be greatly obliged to you.'

Vishnu Sharma smiled at me and said, 'So you say I have to study for fifteen years?'

'It could be done in a few years less, depending on your patience. If a school principal certifies that he trained you, you might enter the eighth grade straight away and skip the first seven years.'

'Can't you do better? Eight years is too long,' said Vishnu Sharma.

'Let me think. There is a way. You can study privately, and take an examination called Matriculation. It is equivalent to twelfth grade. If you pass that, you can do your BA in four years.'

'I cannot avoid school, right?'

'Right. There used to be a way for pandits. But now the rules have changed. Everyone must go to school.'

'What is all this mess? Why should pandits go to school?' said Tikkanna.

I told him pandits are just pandits, ignorant of modern science, history and geography. He was angered by this suggestion. I didn't say a word. Instead, I turned to Vishnu Sharma and said, 'So I can depend on you for helping with the cooking for the three days my wife is out?'

'Not just for three days, three days every month, thirty-six days a year. I am here at least five years to do my BA, right? That adds up to eighty days, a total of about six months that I will cook for you.'

That's fine with me. But the other problem is not resolved. My wife is coming on Wednesday. These people will not take human form until Thursday. How to resolve this crisis?

I had an idea and I told them, 'You know what you can do? Go to the canal bank on Thursday and take your human form there. Then you can come straight to my house as regular people.'

Vishnu Sharma did not like this idea. 'There are people all over that canal bank. If they see two men taking shape in empty space right before their eyes, they will think we are ghosts. And if we come to your house, everyone in the town will say that you have ghosts in the house. That's no fun,' he said. He insisted on taking human form right inside the house.

I am not comfortable with that idea. That will scare my wife out of the house.

So, what do I do? I was stressed out.

'Why do you want to kill me? Leave me alone. Vishnu Sharma, why do you have to learn English? What do you lose if you don't? Is Indra crazy about this language too? He wants to learn it from you, right? O, what a language this is! It can even make the Gods crave it.'

Vishnu Sharma grabbed me and said, 'Come on! What do you want us to do now? Think of something.'

My wife is definitely coming this Wednesday. These people do not become men until Thursday. They cannot take human form in my house, nor out there on the canal bank. Is there a problem like this in the Mahabharata? In the *Pancatantra*?

Five

Some problems look so big you feel like it is the end of the world. You think you are done for. But if God wants to keep you alive, he will show you a simple solution. All that discussion we had was yesterday; it was almost four in the morning. They were probably still talking but I fell asleep. What could they do? They are sleepless beings. By the time I woke up it was nine o'clock. There they are still sitting in front of me. I felt sad for them. They might have been great people while they were alive, but now they are, nothing but balls of air. There is still some hope for them though. At least they are going to live like us for some time. I got up. As my habit goes, I climbed the neem tree to find a good twig to brush my teeth and by the time I was finished with that ritual it was almost ten.

Today is a working day. I have to go to school. I'm getting worried about my coffee and tiffin. I am rushing to get ready when the young man from the neighbour's runs up to me. I fear it is bad news. He comes up to me and says, 'Teacher, teacher, there is no school today.'

'Why my good boy?'

'A student from our school died in a truck accident.'

'I am sorry to hear that,' I said.

He hurried off without waiting to hear my words.

Vishnu Sharma who was listening asked, 'What is a truck?'

'That's a kind of automobile, except it does not transport people.' I told him all about trucks, almost like it was a part of his English lesson.

It's time for my coffee but I'm not going to get them hooked on coffee, no way. I should go into the kitchen, make my coffee and drink it quietly. If they notice, they will ask me what I am drinking. I will have to lie. Serving them coffee day after day is not as easy as teaching them how to spell 'coffee'. I buy this expensive coffee—Indian Coffee—month after month. No lower-grade stuff will do for my wife. You know how she got into this coffee habit? It was after our marriage, but before she came to live with me. One of her brothers used to work in Bombay making forty rupees a month. For our lot, that was a big job. He was working for the railways, so he took his sister free of charge to Bombay. Taking her around the city, and showing her this and that, he took her to India Coffee House and bought her a cup of coffee. That was how it began. That was before Independence. Now even Indian Coffee tastes as stale as any other low-grade coffee, but my wife won't listen.

Anyway, by the time I finished my morning meal, the mailman brought a letter. It was from my wife. May her four children live for a thousand years! She wrote that her aunt's granddaughter has matured (I don't know the girl, and for that matter, my wife's aunt either) and on Wednesday they are celebrating the ball-playing rite. So, she cannot come home on Wednesday; she will leave on Thursday and arrive on Friday. I took the letter to them and read it out loud. They were never so pleased, not even when they were in heaven. The duo was saved. I should include myself in the group and say, the 'three-o' was saved, but you would object that there is no such word. I know, and we keep giving lectures about people like you who object to new words. Now that the problem is resolved, I should begin teaching English to Vishnu Sharma and take Tikkanna out to meet scholars. But they said, 'We cannot learn anything until we acquire human form. Until then we won't be able to unlearn all we know, nor will our minds be sufficiently dull. Only then can we learn what you teach. We have to wait.' There are four days to go— Monday, Tuesday, Wednesday and Thursday. I can't stand these people for so long. I suggested that they go out and visit other places in Andhra. Vishnu Sharma can visit the villages given to him by his king tax-free. And Tikkanna can go to Nellore, his old patron's place. However, Tikkanna spoilt the idea. He said to Vishnu Sharma: 'Ayya! I go back eight hundred years. You are some two or three thousand years older than I am. My Nellore is not the same old town any more. If you go to your villages, you won't find anything you can recognize. I went to Nellore. I could not even recognize the Penna river. They put a belt on her and another decoration as well. There is something across it, not touching the water. And there is a row of boxes running over it. There was nothing that interested me, so I came back. If you go to your villages, they may not even be there any more! Suppose there was a hill close to your village and you want to look for it; it was your landmark. The hill, most probably, is not there any more. People may have dug it up to lay a road through it. If you can recognize your hill from the rocks on the roadside, then you can go. Only if you can do so standing by the side of the street. If you bend closer to look at the rocks, a truck or two will run you over. You won't come back here, no English, no nothing.'

Listening to this harangue, Vishnu Sharma said he wouldn't go. Both of them sat like rocks. How to avoid them? All yesterday I could see them only in my dream, when I was sleeping. But today I see them even when I am awake. So I respectfully said, 'Ayya, you are guests. For another four days you won't have human worries like I have. I have to attend to my work and stuff. I hope you don't mind my leaving you.'

'Go ahead, don't mind us,' said Vishnu Sharma. 'Go attend to your work. We don't need anything, neither food nor drink. We don't mind if you don't even pay attention to us.'

It was a fine thing to say, but how do you ignore people sitting in front of you? Do I have an option? Why not take a leave of absence from work and go to my in-law's house? I remembered that taking a leave of absence is not that easy, so I decided to stay. I had only one worry, though. I'm not a nobody. I have an MA; I am considered an expert in Telugu literature. I am invited all over the country to give talks. However, if these people ask me a question and I cannot answer, they will laugh at me. Actually, I am not very strong in old Telugu. Whenever I had to teach an old text, I went to my colleague, the pandit on our faculty, had him explain the words, and then taught it in the class. What if Tikkanna should ask me the meaning of any of his verses known for their complicated syntax? What if Vishnu Sharma should test me on a verse from his *Pancatantra*? How humiliating it would be to admit that I am no scholar. Well, I do have a weapon to defend myself, actually two. One is the history of literature; the other is philology. They are very powerful weapons. You cannot use them every time. You have to use them as last resorts. They are like nuclear weapons. You use them only to reduce a Japan to its final surrender. I'll use them in due time, there is no rush for it.

As I was sitting there thinking, Vishnu Sharma asked, 'What's that thing you are thinking about, philology?'

God, I can't even think of something in my own mind. They can see everything. Should I or shouldn't I tell them what philology is? What does it matter anyway? So I told them: 'In Germany, in England, great Sanskrit scholars compared Sanskrit, Arabic, Persian, Greek, Latin and other languages and traced their origin and whatnot and wrote volumes. They wrote about when the Vedas were composed, how many times each word was used in the Vedic corpus and so on. They did a lot of work.' Vishnu Sharma was not only left unimpressed, he asked me with a smile, 'So, when were the Vedas composed?'

'Most probably about two thousand years before Christ.'

'What would that be from now?'

'About four thousand years.'

He looked at Tikkanna, who looked at the sky. I was getting very uncomfortable. I asked, 'Why, what do you think? Were not the Vedas composed four thousand years ago?'

Tikkanna said, 'No doubt, it was *before* four thousand years.'

'It would be equally correct to say it was before four million thousand years,' said Vishnu Sharma. 'Once it is in the past time, how does it concern us how far back it was in the past? For example, Rama killed Ravana. What does it matter if he killed him yesterday, or a million years ago? Killed is a verb in the past tense, isn't that enough for the limited purposes of our life on earth?'

If they were to start an argument with me, I would show them internal evidence. That is a huge research area. Determining the date of a particular text is a very complex matter. The precise dates of a lot of authors need to be determined first, and then you go backwards in time to determine the relative priority of texts. In the case of words, we have to investigate which of them were older forms, and which were new and thus determine the time of the text based on that. It is not enough to say it is old.

Tikkanna intervened. 'I know all your thoughts,' he said. 'Do you know why I looked up at the sky when Vishnu Sharma looked at me? All those dates have to be calculated based on the planets. All those other methods you are thinking of in your mind are wrong-headed, fit only for this ignorant age.'

I got upset. 'We too know a thing or two about the planets,' I said with a sense of sarcasm. 'Balagangadhara Tilak and others have not only studied the planets, but have also determined the age of the Vedas. They decided that at most it could be taken back to 10,000 years before Christ. They are not any older.'

Vishnu Sharma said, 'The sky appears as something we can see with our eyes. But, young man, what about time? You only know the present, what do you know about the endless past?'

'You don't know that either,' I said in retort. With this blow, I thought his bones would break and he would stop arguing. I looked at Vishnu Sharma to see if his face had turned blue with shame. No, he looked quite normal. He is all air, I thought, so it would not show on his face.

He said, 'You had a great-great-grandfather, right? He died in his childhood. You had a grandfather. He died in his childhood, too. Your father was born after your grandfather died. What do you say?'

'Your great-grandfather died exactly the same way,' I said with pent-up anger.

'True. We do not know any better than you about
the past. But you've a passionate attachment for your
grandfather. That's why you were upset when we joked
about him. Suppose we are passionately attached to
the Vedas, wouldn't we be upset too? But let us tell you
something. The Vedas are the same for all of us. When the
Vedas are not treated with respect, you should be upset too.
We don't understand why you aren't.'

'How much are you paid?' asked Tikkanna.

'Peanuts, I get about one hundred and fifty rupees, all
allowances included,' I said, wondering why he asked.

'See, you were willing to agree that the Vedas were
written four thousand years ago, for just one hundred and
fifty rupees. Imagine why people who make four or five
thousand rupees a month shouldn't agree. Money talks. If
you agree with all their views, you get your salaries. Or else
they will put you in the category of pandits and pay you
thirty or forty rupees a month.'

It looks like these people came to brainwash me, not to
learn from me, nor to regain fame with my help. I've made
up my mind. I'm not going to change, no matter how hard
they try. I do not want to change. I will not change. Never.
Suppose I went out and said, 'The Vedas are revealed
knowledge; they were not written by human beings.' Do
you think anyone will even look at my face? Would anyone
invite me for a conference again? The press will ridicule
me. No, I am not going to do that. I told myself: I will
appear to agree with these people and criticize modern
ideas, but in public I will take every word written by the

Englishman as the final standard. There is this story about a man who woke up and cried for losing the money found in his dream. I won't be a fool and lose my job for these people. I am thinking of working for my doctorate. I was about to say to them: 'I actually side with you, but in public it's a different story.' Then I remembered that they already knew all my thoughts. So what's the point in lying?

What could I do in this situation? God is being very unfair to me. Before he sent me these kind of people, he should have given me the skill to control my mind. You might say it is possible only for yogis. I am not asking God to make me a yogi. Who wants to be a yogi anyway? What's left if you become a yogi? All you will have is ashes. I must get a big job, get a doctorate, I should be chief professor of my department in the university. That is the real fun. Suppose the Americans ask, 'Who is the greatest man in the Telugu land?' I will say, 'Me.' That news will be published in America. No matter how many people here fret and fume, that will be the stamp of final recognition. Anyway, by the time these people get their human forms, they won't remember a thing.

Just as I was thinking all this, Vishnu Sharma said, 'Young man, you are intelligent. What you think of us is correct. From Thursday on we lose the ability to know your thoughts. You know why? Because we will acquire bodies. A material body naturally produces ignorance.'

I immediately stood up and protested, 'No, I don't agree. Look how many great minds there are among human beings. There's Max Muller, there's Bardwell Keith, there's

Aldous Huxley, and many more. This theory that the material body naturally generates ignorance could only be believed by people like you who believe in the Vedas, the sastras and all those superstitious texts. But this is the twentieth century! Look, there is an explosion of knowledge everywhere. You have seen it even in heaven; one hundred people petitioned Indra that Vishnu Sharma did not really write the *Nīticandrika*. Where did these people come from? From earth, right? This shows that knowledge on earth is growing enormously. What do you say about that?'

Vishnu Sharma, who has an answer for everything, couldn't open his mouth. He quietly agreed and so did Tikkanna.

I jumped with joy and cried, '*Iravayyo satābadam zindābād!* Viva twentieth century!'

Six

My wife came home. We agreed that these two people will stay in our house. Everything was going smoothly because of Vishnu Sharma. He turned out to be a major help for my wife. She calls him with endearing respect, *bābugāru*, father. With his help, my wife's work is reduced to half of what it used to be. The kids used to literally eat her alive. There is something magical about this man, he gathers them around him and tells them stories. They cluster around him like he is their grandfather.

The day after my wife came home, it rained heavily. Our firewood got all wet. The stove was not burning well. It virtually went on strike. Vishnu Sharma went into the kitchen. He must have done something to the stove; it obeyed him like a slave and began to burn; rice, lentils, soup and curry, he cooked them all in a breeze.

Now my wife knew the trick: whenever the stove does not burn well, she says, 'Babugaru, this stove is not behaving again!' Those are the magic words; Vishnu Sharma comes and the cooking is done in five minutes.

Fifteen days passed. I haven't done a thing for either of them. No lecture engagements for Tikkanna, no English lessons for Vishnu Sharma. Tikkanna did not seem to mind. He comes on time, eats and goes his way. But Vishnu Sharma is not happy. He came and said, 'Listen, I slave in your house doing all the work, but you have not even taught me the alphabet yet.'

I couldn't put it off any longer. I got my son's English textbook and my daughter's slate. I showed him the capital letters in the alphabet. He began to learn them. He said he will practise writing them. I said, 'You don't write them, just remember them.'

'Is this a language only for reading and not for writing?' he asked.

'No, it is written too but there is a separate set of letters for that. You don't use these letters for writing. These letters are for printing.'

'Why do you need one for printing and one for writing?'

'You see, it is difficult to print written letters. Print letters are clear and straight. Written letters go round and round. When some people write, you can't see any letters at all. Print letters are easy for reading.'

'You can write the same letters, they take their own curves in writing. Why do you need a different set of letters with different curves?'

'We can't have arguments on the very first day. If this is how you go on, you will never learn. If you promise not to talk until you learn all these letters, I will teach you.'

'Fine.'

I went out to run some errands and returned in the evening.

'Where have you gone? I don't need all this time to learn those stupid letters. Come, bring a book of some sort. We can begin to read.'

'Wait, not so soon. You learnt twenty-six letters; there are twenty-six more. You can't read a book until you learn those too.'

'Twenty-six, plus twenty-six—fifty-two letters! This is a language with a huge syllabary.'

'Not quite. These twenty-six are essentially the same as the ones you have already learnt. They are the "small letters". The ones you've learnt are the "big letters"; they call them capital letters.'

'If they are the same, why do I have to learn them separately? This is like showing me your uncle when he has his shirt on and then with his shirt off? It's the same uncle.'

'Wait a minute. There is a purpose for the "big letters". You have to write them in the beginning of a sentence.'

'Ah, it is like a feast of the royal Velamas. At the beginning of every row of a Velama feast, they seat a panegyrist from the Bhatraju caste. The Bhatraju asks for a second helping and even a third helping of everything without hesitating, and so the Velamas can have it too. They themselves don't ask, they are too proud to do so. These big letters are like Bhatrajus at a Velama feast. These are called capital letters. I get it.'

So I showed him the lower-case letters.

'If these are all letters for printing, are there two sets of letters for writing as well?' he asked.

I said yes, and asked him to memorize the lower-case letters. However great a scholar he might be, he was confused by a different set of letters for the same sounds. He got the capital 'F' just fine, but when it came to the lower-case 'f' he was lost.

'What is this?' he complained. 'You say this is /ef/ and this one is also an /ef/? Come on! Forget that I am Vishnu Sharma who came from heaven. Teach me like you would teach your little son.'

I told him that I was teaching him exactly the way I taught my son. He asked me again if I told my son that every letter had two shapes and that is how he had to remember them.

I said, 'That's exactly what I told him and he listened and learnt; no questions. This is the problem with teaching adults. If you take a dog that can talk to hunt and say sic'em, he says sic'em back to you. You are making such a fuss to learn the alphabet, do you think I can succeed in teaching the rest of the language to you?'

'That's not the point,' he said, 'I am not talking about me. If I don't want to learn, I will leave. But why should all our Telugu kids undergo this suffering?'

The next day I had to follow my usual routine of going to school and all that. I didn't come home until 5.30 in the evening. By the time I came home he had fed the kids, and served supper to Tikkanna and my wife too. I came and ate. The kids were sleeping. I was dead tired after a long day's work in that godforsaken school and was about to go to sleep. I got into bed when he came and asked to be taught. Poor man, he had cooked for the whole family. I ate his food, just lentils and spinach, but my goodness, it was only a notch below heaven. He must have been a cook in his previous life. How could I say 'no'?

I sat up. 'Those letters you learnt are for print,' I said. 'Here are the letters for writing.' I took a sheet of paper and wrote cursive letters, both capitals and lower case.

'You have to learn to write them. If you trace them with this pencil a few times, you will learn to write them,' I said.

'I will worry about writing later. Now I know how to read. So let us start to read a book,' he said.

'It is not that easy,' I explained. 'You need to know a lot of words first. You can't read until then.'

'Why? You learn words as you read.'

'How do you do that?'

'What do you mean how? Take this Telugu poem of Tikkanna's, for instance: *srī 'yana gauri nān baragu cĕlvaku cittamu pallavimpa*. You say: *srī* = goddess Lakshmi, *annan* = called, *gauri* = goddess Parvati, *nān baragu* = *nān* + *paragu* = called, *cĕlvaku* = to the woman—and so on. As you go you stop at the end of each word and give its meaning.'

I thought about what he said. It doesn't work that way in English. Words are spelled differently than they are pronounced. So I told him, 'The nature of this language is different. You have to learn the words first, until then you can't read books.'

He agreed. 'That's why our gurus teach us *Amarakosa, Andhra-nāma-saṅgraha* and such lexicons to begin with. Knowing words helps in reading texts.'

So far so good. I must teach him words. I took my son's book and showed him the first word 'A'. 'This is a word. It means "one",' I told him.

'It is a great language,' he said in admiration. 'It begins with monosyllabic words. This must be a very expressive language. You can create multiple meanings with it.'

'Wait a minute,' I said, 'you are rushing to conclusions. There are only two monosyllabic words. This one and 'I', which means *nenu*. I gave the meaning of the word in Telugu. You should always use a capital letter for that word.'

'What do I need to write this language for? I don't need a job. Let Tikkanna learn to write. He wants to be a professor of Telugu. He probably needs to learn English to do that. He is sleeping over there, wake him up and ask him to come learn with me.'

I went to wake up Tikkanna. He was sleeping on the back porch on a mat. That was the only mat I had, and that too, torn and old, like the poet Gattu Prabhu said, 'an ancient rag, a hundred thousand pieces sewn together'. I pitied the great man, the creator-deity of Telugu poetry, the minster of king Manumasiddhi. Why did these people choose a poor man like me to visit on this earth?

I tried to wake him up. What should I call him? Tikkanna garu?

It is not good manners to call an older person by name. Can I touch him? What would he think if I

shake him to wake him up? We are against treating
the lowest castes as untouchables, but the untouchability
of those who are respectable is not going to go away.
No, I cannot touch Tikkanna. Who is untouchable here,
me or Tikkanna? Anyway, I cannot touch him. I cannot
call him by name. So, I called him, 'O! Creator-god
of Poetry, O! Friend of the two schools of poets! Are
you up?'

He sat up and said he was awake. I said, 'Vishnu
Sharma says that you should learn English too. He says it
would be more useful to you than to him. Why don't you
come? I am teaching him now.'

'Yes, I will, if Vishnu Sharma says so.'

I knew he would respect Vishnu Sharma's advice.
Tikkanna came and sat next to Vishnu Sharma. I asked him
to learn the capital letters of the alphabet, and then I would
start the lesson. Vishnu Sharma gave him a brief introduction
to the alphabet: 'These are the big letters; these the small
letters; twenty-six each. They are called thus not because of
their size; they are their names.' Tikkanna took a good look
at the alphabet. 'Start the lesson,' he said. 'I will learn the
alphabet as we read.'

I was getting sleepy, but I had to go on. I have a lot
of respect for them. However, they don't seem to have
any regard for me. But, I am not ready to let them go
either. Firstly, I can't let go of Vishnu Sharma; he is far
too useful in the house. And Tikkanna, I have yet to make
some money off of him. So I began to teach them. I told
Tikkanna about the letters 'A', and 'I'.

He asked me 'What's the word for second person singular?'

I said, 'You.'

'I see,' he said. 'There is a letter "U" in the alphabet. So, there are three monosyllabic words, not two.'

'No, that's not how it is written. This is how "you" is written.' I showed him the spelling, y-o-u.

'Come on, you are pulling my leg. You write three letters and pronounce only the last one of them? I don't believe any language can be this clumsy. And you say this is a great language. Please teach it to us as it is. No tricks.'

How do I convince them that I am teaching them as it is? I realized that this is a language I can force down the throats of kids but not one I can teach to intelligent adults. I never knew all this time that we pronounce only the last letter of the three letters in 'you'. Is this my knowledge or ignorance? Anyway, I gave them three letters '*b*,' '*a*' and '*d*' and asked them to say '*baed*'. They read the letters *bee*, *ay*, *dee*, but were not willing to read them together. I told them how the word is pronounced: '*baed*'. The way it is written is the order of letters, called spelling in English. I also told them there are many complications in English spelling. 'Please, read these three letters together, *baed*, and I'll explain about spelling later. Learn this first.'

'Now I get it,' said Tikkanna. 'The '*bee*' stands for the sound /b/and the '*dee*' stands for the sound /d/. Am I right?' I felt much relieved.

'So, they are all consonants?' asked Vishnu Sharma.

'I don't think so,' said Tikkanna. "*Ay*" does not sound like a consonant. It has nothing to do with the /ya/ sound, I think it is an /e/.'

'No, it is an /a/ sound,' I clarified.

'Then where is long /a/?' asked Vishnu Sharma.

'It is both long and short,' I said.

Tikkanna was listening with his lower jaw dropped.

'That can't be true. You probably don't know it well enough. The other day you said some word for the Creator, God or something. What is its order of letters?'

'*G-o-d*,' I said.

'That's it,' said Vishnu Sharma turning to Tikkanna. 'If the /a/ is short you write "a", and if it is long you write "o".'

I was getting very uncomfortable. I don't know how I can teach them English. I wondered what planet was dominant in my horoscope, but I had never had such a malignant planet so far.

I said, 'If you want to learn English, you have to unlearn what you know.'

Both of them went to bed.

Seven

Thank God, they did not bother me until Sunday. But they had been talking to each other frequently, and I had a faint idea that it was about the English alphabet. It always helps if two people learn together; one supports the other.

They came to me on Sunday after the midday meal and said, 'You see, the other day we had a discussion about spelling. The last four days we have been thinking about your alphabet. We have a few questions; can we ask you now?'

'Go ahead, ask!' I said.

Vishnu Sharma began. 'Take these two letters, "*bee*", and "*dee*". Let us say the "*ee*" associated with these letters is added for the convenience of pronouncing the consonant. We looked at all the consonants. There are only seven letters with an "*ee*" associated with them: "*bee*", "*gee*", "*cee*", "*dee*", "*tee*" and "*vee*". There are seven more consonants. Why can't they be pronounced with an "*ee*", too? Moreover, why are these letters in this order? Any significance? There are not enough vowels here. There are some letters with no function at all. For example, "*y*". You can have "*v*" with an "*ai*" serve the same role. And then there is this "*q*". What is this for? What consonant does it represent? Tell me, is this a well-thought-out language? Is this a language blessed by God?'

'Ayya, if you ask me, this is the only language blessed by God. No language in the world is spoken by so many people as this one. That in itself is enough to show that God has blessed it.'

'That's not what I mean by God's blessing. But leave that alone, this language is not *samskṛta*,' said Vishnu Sharma.

'What a great discovery! You had to come all the way from heaven to figure it out! Of course this is not Sanskrit, this is English.'

'We didn't say Sanskrit. We said *samskṛta*.'

I did not follow what he meant and putting my pride aside asked, 'What's the difference?'

'A samskṛta language is one which is perfected. Language exists in a perfected form even before it takes utterance. Sanskrit is such a language. It was born perfected. These other languages, you know, have been spoken as wild languages for a long time, with no writing. No great sages create disciplines of knowledge in those languages. At some point of time, these languages acquired a kind of script from their contact with civilized people. Great seers searched in a disciplined state of mind for the source of the first sound, looked inward to see how the indestructible syllable was born, how it got modulated in its path through the lungs, throat, face and was formed into a systematic set of syllables. Sanskrit is perceived in a perfect state by such seers. The English alphabet is a jumble of sounds. This is not revealed knowledge of ordered sounds, what we call *varna-samāmnāya*. Well, we still have to learn it. It is our karma.'

I wondered about my teaching. What kind of teacher am I to these people? I said, 'Ayya, you are great men. You know what you just did? You destroyed the English alphabet. You crushed it with a pestle and mortar, like you would when you make chutney.'

It was evening. The readers might not feel it, but for one who sits before them and answers all their questions, it's torture. I wanted to get out and relax. If I stay home, they will pester me. So I went to a movie. It was a Telugu movie, a full three-and-a-half-hour-long one. By the time I came home everyone was sleeping. I quietly entered the kitchen, served myself some rice and curry and ate. Just as I was going to get some buttermilk from the shelf above, the ladle hit the pot and made a clanking sound. My wife woke up and came into the kitchen. I put my finger on my lips and said, 'Shhh, don't talk,' and quietly went to bed.

The next morning my wife asked, 'Why did you hush me up last night, what was the matter?'

'You know I have been teaching our guests; I am getting sick of teaching them. I went to the movies last night to escape. I was quiet because I did not want to wake them. If they woke up, they would kill me with their questions.'

She asked, 'What movie did you go to?'

I was caught. It was a mistake to mention the movie. She would ask me why I went to a movie without her. I promised I would take her when I got paid. At the moment I don't have money for her, the kids and two guests. She quietly said, 'We are out of rice and ghee.' Today is the twenty-third. I don't get paid until the first. Where will I get money now?

As they say in English, necessity is the mother of invention.

I thought of arranging the first lecture for Tikkanna at my school. At noon, when the faculty was taking their lunch break, I gathered the Telugu faculty and a few others who have a liking for Telugu, and gave them a speech: 'I suppose you know that two Brahmin men are staying at my house for the past fifteen or twenty days,' I began. 'This is a secret of the gods. No one believes it in this day and age, but I am telling you the truth—I would not tell you if you were like those Western-minded people, but you are Telugu teachers, you have a love for the Telugu language, that's why I am telling you. Among those two—the man who has lighter skin, is tall and has striking features, bright eyes—that man is Tikkanna.

'This is the very man who wrote the Mahabharata,' I continued. 'He came to my house in his own person. The other man is—you know Vishnu Sharma who wrote the *Pancatantra* in Sanskrit—that's him. By some fate, they were cursed by the gods to spend time on earth. Believe it if you will, or even if you don't, they are good scholars. We can have a lecture by them. There is money in the student union fund to give them a little honorarium. What do you say?'

Some faculty showed a little excitement. A few were indifferent. But no one was opposed to the idea. I started a list of donations. Some thirty rupees were pledged. I went to the principal. Fortunately, he is a theosophist. When I said that Tikkanna visited me, he agreed that this was entirely possible. What more did I need? He pledged fifty rupees from the college fund.

My goodness, Tikkanna is covering an entire month's expenses with one lecture. That's Tikkanna. Let any of these modern poets do that! Let them bring not eighty, just fifteen rupees. I know. It felt like I had fallen into a breadbasket.

Now I can make money using Tikkanna. Apart from that, I can buy rice and ghee this evening.

I came home. I told Tikkanna, 'Ayya, we arranged a meeting for you at my school this evening. The student secretary of the Literary Association will come to fetch you at 4.30 p.m. Please come to the school with him.' Vishnu Sharma asked if he could come too. 'Please do,' I said. 'You could speak too.'

'What do you want me to talk about?' Vishnu Sharma asked, and without waiting for my answer continued, 'I will talk about your English alphabet. I will tell them there isn't a rottener syllabary in this whole world. Would you like me to do that?'

'God no, don't do that. Our principal is a theosophist. That's why he believed you came from heaven. However, for theosophists, English is greater than their mother tongue. If you abuse English, we not only lose the money we are getting today, he will be mad at me for bringing you to the school. I might even lose my job. Please don't do that. Tell them some stories; the students will like them.'

At 4.30 in the afternoon, the secretary went and brought the two guests in a rickshaw. Both of them were wearing light-red dhotis. Let alone jackets, they didn't even have shirts on. They came with a piece of cloth on their shoulders, like the poor Brahmins who sell snuff at the Siva temple. It didn't occur to me that they do not have decent clothes to wear until I saw them at the school. The first thing I should do with the money from this meeting is to buy them decent clothes.

They came and sat on the dais. The meeting hall was crowded. Usually no one shows up at these meetings, except when government ministers come. The audience at the literary lectures is usually small—a few students who specialize in Telugu, four to be exact, and we, the Telugu faculty. Today every student in the college was here. Maybe they heard that these people were visitors from heaven.

Our principal presided over the meeting. He got up and began his remarks. He speaks a kind of English, old and well preserved, like pickled lemon. He is a theosophist, right? So, he dug up all those ideas—astral bodies, esoteric knowledge and so on. No one was listening. The audience was busy talking among themselves. Finally, he said, 'Now Tikkanna will speak.'

Tikkanna stood up. The audience was still. He read this well-known poem from his Mahabharata: *siṅgamb'ākaṭito guhāntaramunan*. He read with an elongated voice. His tone has a strangely rough quality, with a bit of an accent. The poem was melodious though. His voice deep, like a thundering cloud.

The trouble, however, was that our kids only like the movie music. They have a favourite singer who sings verses in the movies; they like the verse only if you sing it like the movie singer. They won't listen to anyone else, even if he should come from heaven. They started making catcalls.

Tikkanna concluded his talk and sat down. Then Vishnu Sharma stood up. Seeing that he looked like a bear, they started making sounds like so many animals in the jungle. Students in these schools are very smart, except of course, in their studies. One of them began to growl just like a forest bear. How many people know that a bear sounds like that? Only a couple of students come from forest areas but within minutes everyone began to growl exactly like that. I wondered if they came to school straight from the jungle.

Suddenly something unexpected happened. Vishnu Sharma himself began to growl like them. Amazed, everyone looked at him. He stopped for a second and said, 'Not just growling like a bear, I can roar like a lion, too.' And he roared like a lion. The students were totally smashed.

'I wrote the *Nīticandrika* in which all the animals talk,' he continued. 'I know how animals communicate. I know their languages. I know how they make sounds. I can make all those sounds.'

He made the sounds of ten different animals. The audience was spellbound.

I went into the audience to collect donations. Believe me—there were sixteen hundred students, some of them from very rich families—how much do you think I collected? I held my paper like a plate that goes round after a Purana performance, didn't I? Nine hundred fifty-nine rupees, ten annas and four paise. The principal gave the fifty he promised. The faculty will pay at the end of the month. We headed home. By the time we got there, my kids—I wonder how they knew—stood at the front door shouting, '*Vishnu Sharma ki jai*, viva Vishnu Sharma!'

Eight

The news spread like wildfire. The townspeople began to talk, each in their own way.

'They really came from heaven. Show me any person like these two. They look like people walking on wind. They are not really human,' said some.

Yet others said, 'It is true. We went close and touched them. We didn't feel their bodies; it didn't feel like touching a human being.'

Still others said, 'This is a very clever plan. He made one thousand rupees in one hour. In a few months, he is going to net twenty-five, thirty thousand. After that why would he need this teaching job? He will go into business.'

'People are fools,' said a smart person. 'They believe, even in these days, that men come down from heaven. In this country, people believe anything.'

I took them to the shop and bought them two first-class dhovatis and two long uttarīyams. I had silk shirts tailored for them, and had two cots and mattresses made. I bought two woollen shawls and bought handspun dhovatis and shirts as well, just in case they need to see a minister or such person in public office. I told them that these clothes are meant for formal occasions, and not for everyday use at home. I told them one thing more.

'Ayya, when we go to meetings, you should shave. These days, you are considered a village lout if you don't shave. In English they call such a person a brute. You have to consent to this requirement.'

Vishnu Sharma looked sideways. Tikkanna did not say anything. He was used to royal courts. He must shave every day. But Vishnu Sharma said, 'What is this nuisance? I won't let a barber touch me except on proper days.'

'You don't have to,' I said. 'I have a safety razor.' He asked me for more information about it. I gave him the words and their spellings. I showed him my razor.

'It doesn't cut into your skin,' I assured him. 'That's what is meant by "safety" in the name of the razor.' But then as I was shaving that morning to demonstrate how it works, I cut my face in a couple of places. He laughed. What could I do? I didn't name it safety razor. The people who sold it to me did.

Soon Sunday came. After the meal, both of them came asking for a lesson. I told them frankly, 'Ayya, you should stop bothering me about spelling. No more questions about the alphabet. I will give you some words. You just have to learn them. If you ask questions like, "Why do you write g-e-o-r-g-e when it should be j-a-r-j," I can't teach you. Let me tell you something: Any English letter sounds as it wishes in any place; it does not obey your wishes. I can only teach if you agree to this. Is that clear?'

Tikkanna agreed. He was a diplomat; he knew how to do business. But this Vishnu Sharma had questions.

'There is always a new word. How do you know how to pronounce it? One's learning of this language never ends.'

I said, 'You are right. After so many years of learning the language, we still don't know how to pronounce some words. When an Englishman comes and gives a speech, and pronounces some words in a different way from the way we have done so far, we begin to pronounce those words as he pronounced them. Until recently we said *le ba re ta ri*, now we say lĕboratori. Moreover, there are some French words. That's an even more civilized language. The words in that language have four or five letters at the end, all of which have to be uttered in a puff. No rhyme or reason.'

They agreed to the condition. I picked up my son's first-grade book.

Each lesson has a list of new words in the beginning. I wrote some forty words from that list on a piece of paper with their pronunciation and meaning. I did a smart thing yesterday—I haven't yet told you about it. I bought a sheet of carbon paper. Now I made two copies of that list, gave it to them and asked them to read. My plan is to give these words for their homework and go to the movies with my wife and kids. By the time we come back it will be close to midnight. They will be fast asleep. Ever since I bought the cots, mattresses and woollen blankets, they have been sleeping soundly—literally—making a lot of sounds. You should hear them when they snore. It is like the frogs in the Rig Veda. I gave them the list of words and told my wife to get ready to go to the movies.

That's it, a whole new story began. By the time she bathed the four kids, combed their hair—two of the little bastards only have short hair—and dressed them in clean clothes—it was five o'clock. My fear was that the two monsters might turn up in half an hour and say they have memorized all those words and ask for a new lesson. One way to escape from teaching a new lesson was to quiz them on the words; but how could I test people of their status? One wrote the Mahabharata and the other is the author of *Pancatantra*! After all, there were hardly forty words. For people who have gobbled up huge disciplines, forty words are hardly enough for a bite.

I kept hurrying my wife. My little girl was the hardest of all. Her mother wanted to dress her in a cotton shirt. My little girl wanted the silk shirt from the dresser. Her mother said that the silk shirt was for festive occasions, not for daily wear. The little one began to cry. It was fine that she cried, only that there was *kāṭika* on her eyes. Who wears kāṭika these days anyway? I told her not to put kāṭika on her eyes but my wife wouldn't listen. She insisted that the kāṭika would make her eyes grow bigger. Who knows whether it does or not. When she cried, all the kāṭika got smudged on her face. Her face had to be washed in a hurry. She used soap but the soap did not clean it, it made it even more smudgy. She had to rub her face with *kuṅkuḍukāya*. The girl was already wearing a clean shirt, right? Being in a hurry, she used the hem of her shirt to wipe her face. Now the shirt was all dirty. So in the end, her mother had to give her the silk shirt anyway. When the kids were dressed, my wife began her make-up. By the time it was all done, it was six o'clock, too late for the movies. But after all we had gone through, we were going anyway.

Meanwhile Vishnu Sharma came and said, 'I memorized all those words.

You look like you are going out with your wife and kids. By the time you come back we will be sleeping.'

I got the hint but said, 'We will have a lesson tomorrow night.'

The next night we were reading under the dim light of a kerosene lamp. I gave him forty words and thought that I could give them a little test. I started with an apology, 'Ayya, you shouldn't mind this. I want to test you to check if you know all the words, spellings and their meanings.' They agreed they should be tested. I asked for the spelling and meaning of 'the'. They answered correctly. Vishnu Sharma asked if the word 'the' meant 'one' and if the word 'a' meant the same. If so, what's the difference between 'a' and 'the'? I said I wasn't sure.

After some discussion about word formation, Vishnu Sharma asked me about the case system in English, 'Tell me what the accusative case is.'

I said there is no accusative case. Moreover, the case is not indicated by a suffix as in Sanskrit and Telugu. English has prepositions.

'You don't have an accusative in English? Then in English how would you say: *rāmuḍu rāvaṇuni campěnu?*'

I gave the translation for the Telugu sentence: Rama killed Ravana.

'I see, but why did you put killed in the middle? The one who is to be killed is free to escape if he is at the very end of the sentence.'

I didn't understand. He explained: 'You say, "Rama killed" but as soon as you say kill, suppose Ravana ran away, who is left to be killed? You have to bring a dog or a goat in his place. But suppose you have Ravana already in the sentence before you utter the verb, he is stuck, he can't go anywhere; he *has* to die.'

'Ayya, enough of these jokes.'

'This is not a joke' said Tikkanna, who was quiet all the while. 'This is about language. A language has to follow the inner movements of the mind and its syntax should support it. When you say the word "killed", the listener should already know who was killed. Knowing it later puts a burden on the delicate movement of the mind. We haven't learnt much of this language yet, but by the time we finished the alphabet, learnt a few words and began to make sentences, we could already see how ridiculous this language is. And you are forcing this language down the throats of kids in this great country, a country where Sanskrit was born, the land where Telugu is spoken? You don't seem to understand how their delicate mental movement is burdened by enforcing this language on them. That's probably why your intelligence is so radiant!'

Vishnu Sharma asked for the instrumental case. I said English uses the preposition 'by' as in 'by the man', 'by the lion' and so on. He asked again, 'Do you say "by the man" or "by man"?' I wasn't sure. Darn it, I studied English for a good quarter of a century, and I am not sure of the use of this 'the'. There are easily some sixty teaching faculty and at least four or five of them think they are very competent scholars of English. One refers to Fowler's dictionary, another refers to the best of encyclopedias. They constantly argue among themselves. There are dozens of books on the correct usage of English. But no one knows for sure where to use the 'the'.

I said, 'Whether you use "the" or not, "by" goes before the noun.'

'All right, I trust you. But try telling your son to do so.'

'Ayya, the trouble is that you already know the grammars of Sanskrit and Telugu. That's why you have so many questions. We just make our kids, who don't know any grammar, repeat "by the cat", "by the dog", "by the man", and so on blindly until it becomes a habit. They can't be bothered to ask what the root is, which the suffix is. They just learn English. Millions of people have learnt that way.'

'Young man, you passed your MA. You think you are a scholar in English, Telugu and Sanskrit. Yet, you don't know the correct use of 'the' in English and we've been observing how much Sanskrit and Telugu you know. Are all the people who claim to know English in this country like you? You do not know English, and neither do you know your Telugu. If you know your mother tongue with its grammar, you can learn any other language easily. I will learn your English in four months. If you spend twenty years in learning a foreign language, without learning your own language, what do you gain? You know neither your mother tongue, nor your mother-in-law's tongue.'

I felt that if I kept quiet, I would lose my power. So I said, 'Ayya, there are lots of people here who have been saying that we should not learn English, that it is no good for us. We don't need you to come all the way from heaven to say that.'

'I am not saying you should not learn English. Indra himself sent me to learn it, and he wants to learn it from me. You know the proverb: win your home before you try to win the court.'

I am getting sick of these people. I cannot help sleeping. Once I sleep, I dream and these people appear in my dream. So, I made a contract with the Monkey God of Macavaram, that if these two people stop coming into my dreams, I will offer him one hundred coconuts. When I told Vishnu Sharma of the contract, he said, 'It is a very expensive contract. One hundred coconuts is a lot of money. Why don't you fulfil your vow in the dream itself? You have that money in the bank, don't you? You won't have it when you wake up. So spend it now.'

I went to the market with them, bought one hundred coconuts, and bargained with a rickshaw driver to carry them. It wouldn't be right to ask Tikkanna to help carry them. And they were too heavy for Vishnu Sharma and me. The rickshaw man asked for one rupee. He is only a dream rickshaw man, right? He could agree for less. But still he wanted a rupee. I paid him and got the coconuts to the temple and fulfilled my vow.

I started to go home. These two were still following me. I asked them, 'Why are you still here? I paid my vow to get rid of you. Go.'

'You don't seem to understand the secret of dreams. It is you that is not leaving us. This is something deeply inscribed in your inner self. Until it is resolved, your mind will keep on dreaming us.'

I have to go on teaching these people. I can't give up.

Nine

These dreams are strange. Sometimes I know I am about to dream. Normally one would not know one was dreaming, until one is awake. For me, however, there was an occasional awareness that I was dreaming even as I was dreaming. Again, there was also a feeling of certainty—right during a dream—that I was not dreaming, that it was real and I was fully awake.

One day, as I was just beginning to see that a dream was coming, the two of them came and sat down. Vishnu Sharma was chewing betel. I don't chew betel. We don't even allow betel nut in my house. I only buy some betel leaves and nuts for the occasion of the anniversary of my father's death. Some time back I used to buy pre-packed betel from the shop instead of fresh betel leaves and nuts to give them to the Brahmins at the ceremony. Once my uncle came to the ceremony and saw me do this. He yelled at me: 'You westernized impure fellow! You and your bastard acts! You say you passed your MA. You should be

135

ashamed of yourself. Who gave you this idea of buying pre-packed betel?'

From then on, I have been buying fresh betel leaves. But anyway, I wondered where Vishnu Sharma got his betel from. I did not ask him though. Tikkanna looked rather cross. I asked him what was wrong.

Tikkanna wanted lecture engagements and I had not done anything about them since I was spending my time teaching English to Vishnu Sharma.

So I told Tikkanna, 'Ayya, when I arranged a lecture for you at my school, you recited just one single poem from your Mahabharata. Your style wasn't quite like ours. It was more like the Nellore style. Your pronunciation was about seven hundred years old. The audience could not relate to your speech pattern. We are using the same Telugu you wrote in your Mahabharata but somehow you sound different when you speak. I didn't know if we should have another lecture for you in the city auditorium or in the library. Anyway, I did arrange a talk for you in the city auditorium. Get ready and we'll go.'

Vishnu Sharma did not move. I asked him if he did not want to go.

'No, I don't,' he said. 'He will fail to please the audience and I will have to make all those funny animal sounds to make the lecture a success. I don't like it.'

'No, you don't have to. I promise I won't ask you to.'

'If you don't, the audience will. I have seen how an audience behaved in a theatre. There was this play: *The Victory of the Pāṇḍavas*. Of all the people, Narada appeared in the play. I wondered what Narada was doing in a Mahabharata play and asked Tikkanna. He said he didn't know; he didn't write the play. Of course, I knew that. But did Narada appear even once in the Mahabharata written by Vyasa?

'Tikkanna was not sure. Maybe, he came when Krishna was negotiating peace with the Kauravas. A large group of sages was present at that time. Anyway, he came. His hair was pressed into shape like the moustache of a white soldier. What kind of a sage was he? He entered and was about to say something to Duryodhana but the audience wouldn't let him. They demanded that he sing a particular song—totally unrelated to the play—and he had to sing it. Your audience's wishes are commands. It could be Narada or it could be me—we must obey their commands or we are dead.[5] I am not ready to die again. I don't want to come to the meeting.'

Tikkanna assured him that things will be better this time. This audience would be different. So Vishnu Sharma came. We went to the meeting. Tikkanna spoke for three hours and the audience listened in pin-drop silence.

Tikkanna said that he would dictate his commentary on all fifteen chapters of his Telugu Mahabharata and that I should be his scribe. That will be the fruit of his appearance in my dreams and that I should publish it.

The idea was great but I was not ready to undertake that kind of burden. Who will buy it these days and what's there in it for me? So I said, 'Ayya, there are still places for us to visit. We should go to Guntur. That is your ancestral town, right? And we should also visit the Andhra University. We will write the commentary later.'

We went to Guntur. No one knew that once upon a time Tikkanna had lived there. I couldn't go from house to house to spread the word, so I printed leaflets and had them distributed. The meeting was held in the College Hall. Unexpectedly, there was trouble at the meeting. Someone brought a rather well-known portrait of Tikkanna which hung in that hall. It was a large colour painting. They brought the painting and asked why Tikkanna did not look like the painting. His identity was now brought into question. I said the painting did not look like Tikkanna. They did not agree, they said that Tikkanna did not look like the painting. It grew to be a real fight. I quietly scratched Tikkanna's back. He and I escaped through a back door and went straight to the train station. A huge group of people followed us crying: 'Kill the pseudo Tikkanna! Death to the impostor!'

We got home safe. I must get Tikkanna's Mahabharata printed with his commentary. At least the first volume. His handwriting should be photocopied and recorded in it. That would be incontrovertible evidence of Tikkanna's identity. I was getting ready to go to Nellore with him. But he was not enthusiastic. 'Enough of this,' he said. 'In Guntur we almost got killed. Nellore might be our death. Instead of all these journeys, why don't you read my Mahabharata? I will teach it to you with my commentary.'

'O Creator of Poetry, you have no idea of Nellore. The people there will receive us with royal honours. Listen to me. Let's go to Nellore.'

He agreed after some persuasion. We went. I gave a press notification ahead of time: 'Tikkanna has come from heaven. He is visiting Nellore on this day.' The train station was teeming with people. They garlanded him heavily, so heavily that his head was covered in flowers. In a way it was good. Should there be a person in this town who claims he has seen Tikkanna before, and if he comes and says this was not Tikkanna, we would be undone. Tikkanna was taken in a procession in a motor car. There was music. Even the Muslims in town walked in front shouting, 'Long Live the Creator of Poetry! Long live the Friend of Both Schools of Poets!'

We went to the meeting. Tikkanna was seated in a huge chair. There were many rich people in the town who had great respect for Tikkanna. They were also seated on the dais. The flood of tributes began. One person after another came and read a long-winded tribute in convoluted Sanskrit phrases. There was no end to it. It was late in the night by the time the reading of tributes was done. It was too late for Tikkanna to speak. So they postponed the proceedings for the next day.

We came to the place where we were to rest for the night. They gave us some food. Tikkanna and I slept on the terrace. Tikkanna did not want to stay in Nellore any longer. He said the atmosphere was no good. The town is split into two factions. You had to belong to one or the other to survive. No one cared for poetry. So we left early in the morning, before anyone woke up.

The newspapers were full of negative talk. He was not Tikkanna. It was impossible for a person to return from heaven. This was an impostor. All hell broke loose against me. Everyone said I was behind this fraud.

We still wanted to go to Andhra University at Visakhapatnam. We went to the campus. I introduced Tikkanna to the students and faculty. No one cared. They said, 'Go to that Telugu department over there.' We went to see the chairman of the department. He was not in the office. We went to the other faculty. One of them invited us to his office. After I introduced Tikkanna to him, he waited a second and said to Tikkanna, 'You used the word *niscintaga* in your Mahabharata. Is it not wrong? The correct form should be *niscintamugā*, right?' Tikkanna was furious at this. I quietly led the way; Tikkanna followed me out.

We returned home. Tikkanna insisted that I should take instructions from him. He will dictate his commentary to his Mahabharata. I must publish the text with *his* commentary.

I said, 'No one would believe that you dictated the commentary in my dream. In fact, no one believes now that God Hari-hara-natha appeared to you in your dream and asked you to write the Mahabharata.[6] There is no point in wasting your time here. Better get back to heaven.'

Vishnu Sharma who was trying to sleep asked me, 'How do you spell enough?' I said: '*E-n-o-u-g-h*.'

He started muttering '*gh*', '*gh*'.

I woke up to his coughing.

Ten

When I came home, Vishnu Sharma said, 'I don't feel like staying here any more. I want to go back. How much more of the grammar is left? Why don't we finish it?'

'Are you kidding? You haven't even learnt half of a mustard seed compared to a pumpkin. What do you know? You know the alphabet and perhaps twenty words. And you want to learn the rest of the language by yourself?'

'I will use the lexicon to find out the verb roots and nouns.'

I laughed. 'What lexicon?' I asked.

'A lexicon like the *Amarakosa*. All the words related to the gods are in the divinity class. It is the same with the earth class and so on.'

I said, 'I really pity you; you are very naive. Even with the little English you know, you should be able to guess that there is nothing in common between us and them. Their dictionaries are not divided into classes. They are in alphabetical order. That means all the words beginning with A are in one place and then the words beginning with B and so on. Man and monkey will be in the same section, one is not in the human class and the other in the animal class. They are all together.'

'All right then, teach me the indeclinables.'

I taught him the few that I could think of. He then asked me about pronouns. I told him that a pronoun is so called because it comes in place of a noun.

'What do you mean it comes in place of a noun?'

'It's used as a substitute for a noun, isn't it?' I gave him an example: 'Rama killed Ravana. He also killed Kumbhakarna.'

'You went to Rajahmundry. You also went to the university. What noun does "you" replace in these sentences?'

I did not know what to say. I wondered what noun that pronoun substitutes? He is talking to me, calling me 'you'. It is not a substitute for my name. My name is not even mentioned. Vishnu Sharma explained: 'If a pronoun is defined as replacement for a noun, "you" and "I" are not pronouns. We call them *sarvanāmas* in Sanskrit meaning names common to all. Everyone can call himself 'I', and anyone you are talking to is 'you'. Any person you talk of is a 'he' or 'she'. That's what a sarvanāma is. This language, English, does not have conceptual purity. I told you before this is some kind of a tribal language. Somehow it has acquired superiority. It acquired some literature, a grammar and things like that from other civilized languages.'

'What do you lose? You say all these words, and go and sit in heaven. If I say these things, I am dead.'

I must have turned pale as I said this. Looking at me Tikkanna said, 'Don't turn so pale. No matter how pale you look, you are not going to be a white man. No matter how much English you speak, you are a black man. Look at the people in Africa. They were not considered white even when they accepted the white man's religion.'

'It doesn't look like you want to continue learning English,' I said to Vishnu Sharma.

He nodded in acceptance.

'As you like,' I said.

I knew he wanted to return to heaven. But I still wanted Tikkanna to stay. I had thought of his desire to teach me his Mahabharata with his commentary. I have cherished a secret hope that I could publish it as my own interpretation.

Tikkanna read my thoughts. 'It doesn't make any difference to me if you want to publish my commentary as your work,' he said. 'But I have given up the idea of commenting on the Mahabharata. I saw the scholars here when you took me to the university. They don't need the beauties of poetry, nor the tradition of interpretation. They think what they do is right. That's how they are born, that's how they have to die. We have to go.'

I put them on a train to Madras but then began to wonder: 'Why did they go on a train? Is there a train to heaven? Who knows where they are travelling from Madras? Maybe to Stalingrad, maybe New York. From there they will probably find room on a rocket or something to the moon. They'll find their way.'

Well, they're gone.

Though I almost miss them.

Soon I woke up. Where was I? I must have slept all night on the porch.

The college peon brought a letter for me. I have been appointed head of my department. Why not? I have dreamt such a great dream. But you know why I got the promotion? Didn't I worship the Monkey God of Macavaram with a hundred coconuts, be it in a dream? That's why.

Afterword

In this essay, I intend to take a closer look at the two novellas for the meaning one can derive out of them as literary works in a postcolonial context and beyond.

Ha Ha Hu Hu: A Horse-Headed God in Trafalgar Square

The principal tone of *Ha Ha Hu Hu* is wonder. A number of synonyms for wonder occur throughout the narrative: the people of London are *surprised* to see the strange creature with a horse's head and a man's body; they are *amazed* to hear it speak. Every act of the animal, every word, provokes a sense of wonder, amazement, marvel. Wonder is a quality of the child, the ignorant and the colonized native.

Yet from the point of view of the gods who by definition know everything, there is nothing which can surprise them. This is evinced in the behaviour of the gandharva. He is never surprised by anything. Neither the great achievements of English industrial culture nor the major inventions of European scientists elicit in him even a mild word of curiosity. A dichotomy is created between knowledge and ignorance, wisdom and innocence, gods and men.

The story depicts a situation that delights Indian nationalists, in which Indian tradition finds a competent spokesman in the mythical gandharva. In the centre of the Emperor's city, the gandharva speaks Prakrit because the common folk do not understand Sanskrit, which is fit only for gods; the British are not sacred enough to be addressed in Sanskrit. Sanskrit scholars from the University of London and from other centres of learning in Europe, who understand the gandharva's Prakrit, a low-class dialect of Sanskrit, are the mediators between sacred Sanskrit and profane English. They are the counterparts of the English-educated Hindu natives who mediated between the King's English and the commoner's Sanskrit. The situation may be represented by the following diagram:

The Brahminic World

SACRED	Sanskrit	European Sanskrit Scholar	English	PROFANE

The Colonial World

ROYAL	English	Hindu English Professor	Sanskrit	COMMON

By virtue of their acquaintance with Sanskrit, the European mediators acquire an aspect of the sacred condition, though their birth still disqualifies them from promotion to the full heights of sacredness. The same is also true of Indians who learnt English; their knowledge of English qualified them for second-level positions in the British bureaucracy, but their birth disqualified them from elevation to the top levels of their administration. And yet, both groups of mediators represent the superior status of their masters when they are in proximity to people of their own race. Once the English had left, English-educated Indians functioned very much as the English had and began to enjoy the status which had been denied them for so long by their imperial masters. They acted as the chief defenders, interpreters and eulogizers of English culture, style and language. Similarly, in Satyanarayana's story, the European Sanskrit scholars act very much like Brahmins who defended Sanskrit culture and traditional attitudes from the onslaught of British culture and learning. They protect Sanskrit culture against the attack of the empiricist professors of zoology and linguistics and guard the gandharva against the people who treat him as an animal.

From another perspective, the European Sanskrit scholars stand in sharp relief against their counterparts in India. They contrast with the English-trained Indian scholars who rejected Sanskrit. The praise and defence of Brahmin culture and learning which is offered by the scholars of the imperial race serve to remind the Indians that in their rejection of Sanskritic learning and in their eagerness to espouse Western ways, they have missed the most valuable part of their own culture.

Similarly, everything that the gandharva and the European Sanskrit scholars do serves a dual purpose for the Indian readers: Their words and actions devalue the British culture and learning and elevate the status of Brahmin culture and learning. Further, they restore the pride and sense of superiority which Brahmin traditionalists had lost, and repair the damage done to their egos. The lifestyle of the gandharva, his way of eating, bathing, meditating and dressing constitute not just a different—in this case, Brahminical—cultural code, but a superior racial style as well. He bathes before eating, he meditates, he eats only fruit, he drinks water from a chĕmbu (a round vessel popularly used by Brahmins in Andhra to drink water). His clothes are not sewn; he has one piece of cloth around his loins and another around his shoulders. He wears gold ornaments on his hands and feet, and since he is a gandharva, a crown on his head as well.

These symbols have two different significations for Hindus and the British. To the Hindus, the dress adheres to the traditional Brahminical style. Of the two pieces of material on his body, a Hindu reader—in this case, a Telugu speaker—readily recognizes that the one tied around his waist is the dhovati and the one draped over the shoulders is the kaṇḍuvā. The gold ornaments, especially the crown and the bracelets with their lion insignia, indicate a person of high birth. This dress style, along with the ritual observances of taking a bath every day, meditation, breath control and vegetarianism, were going out of fashion in India, for they were considered signs of backwardness to English-educated Indians. Likewise, the use of the chĕmbu as a vessel for liquids was replaced by the glass, called in Telugu *glasu*, a loan word from English.

The Enlightenment, which enshrined reason in place of belief, made man the centre of the universe as the only creature endowed with reason; and trust in man's ability to resolve all problems through science unequivocally made him the master of the universe.

When the linguist and the zoologist insisted on cutting open Ha Hu's head to investigate how he could speak, they knew that their actions might endanger Ha Hu's life, but they believed he was an animal and, therefore, were not bothered by ethical considerations. The Sanskritists insisted, on the other hand, that Ha Hu was human, and not an animal. However, Ha Hu's declaration that we are all animals intrigued them.

When Ha Hu was taken to visit the zoo, the animals recognized him as one of their own and became aware of their captivity. They tried to escape. The gandharva could create music, and music could reconnect the broken bond between man and nature.

The gandharva's strength is in the Brahmin's *shastric* point of view that knowledge is inborn and that the only way to gain truth is by turning inward. Study of the external world does not lead to knowledge; it only provides us with useless information, whereas ultimate wisdom is gained through contemplation, *tapas*. The gandharva has no use for research or scientific exploration. He insists:

Why do you people want to research everything? It doesn't look as if you focus your minds to find the truth of things. How much can you know through mechanical means? If you see with a totally focused mind you will find answers.

This brings us to the point made at the beginning of this essay, that wonder is the principal tone of the story. Only ignorant human beings wonder. Gods and others who know everything do not.

Beyond Humanism?

Two questions are left unanswered in the story. Why did the gandharva fall to earth in London? How was he able to fly again? Obviously the music of the piano restored the gandharva's lost powers. Of the whole range of products of civilization that he is shown, the only object in which he shows any interest is the piano. In an otherwise contaminated culture which alienates man from Nature with its extensive mechanization, man's ability to make music is the last humanizing power which is left unaffected. If it were man's ability to create music that renewed the gandharva's power to fly, it must have been something contrary to that that caused him to lose his power in the first place. Although the story remains silent on this detail, one is tempted to speculate that it was London's industrial pollution that robbed the gandharva of his power to fly.

Modern rational man thinks within the framework of two categories: human and non-human. All accepted codes— social, ethical and legal—operate within this framework, in which values and punishments are determined differently for human and non-human categories. According to this system, the uncrowned monarch of the universe is the human being, who also controls the rest of the universe and for whom alone the universe exists. The human being is the only one free to determine what is right and what is wrong, and all other life, though biologically accepted as living, is nevertheless incapable of that.

In the context of a neat, bipartite division of the universe, the appearance of a compound being, half man and half animal, is terribly disturbing, not simply because it is strange, but more fundamentally because it threatens the basic assumptions of the rational and humanistic world view. The question the scientists ask the doctor, 'Do you think he's a man?' sums up the major concern of the culture. If he is not a man, then there are no ethical, social or legal questions to worry about. They may do as they please to investigate his body.

The division of the universe into two parts, human and non-human, does not just separate, but goes so far as to alienate man from the world of which he is a part. As man plays the role of master, attempting to control the rest of the world, he is only alienating himself from his own nature, which he actually shares in common with all beings. This alienation becomes so deep-rooted that the presence of one composite being who is at the same time god, man and animal, disturbs even linguistic categories (it/he). In many places, the text switches nouns and pronouns from human to non-human in a rather confused way to emphasize the discomfort that language experiences in dealing with a phenomenon that does not conform to its grammatical classification.

While Ha Hu is presented to the public, and the scientists, as a monster, it cannot be forgotten that Ha Hu is also all the while observing the people around him. For the colonizer, the colonized subject is somehow subhuman, and as such, a fit subject for display, caged as an animal. Feared, all right, but under proper controls they are objects to be studied and displayed. The gandharva, however, refuses to submit to this perception of the colonizer. He, in his own way, has been observing them, and in the end comes out victorious, diagnosing their problems. In some sense, the gandharva's uncanniness that makes him a fitting object of study for the colonizers, is precisely what makes him something of a superior being, judging and evaluating them in turn. The colonizer remains all too human, and the gandharva, who represents the colonized, is superhuman. The tables are turned; the colonizer has nothing to teach and a lot to learn.

Nature versus Culture

The double-gaze discussed above, between the gandharva and the British also disturbs the nature–culture dichotomy. At this level the message of the story is clear.

There is a fundamental disharmony between Nature and Culture. The disharmony only grows to disturbing proportions when left to the methods of rational thinking. It is only through mediation by the gods that the opposition between man and his world can be transformed into a joyous participation. By emphasizing the shared experiences between gods, men and animals, Satyanarayana depicts an ideal world in which there is interdependence and interaction between all beings. The philosophical discourses by the gandharva may, in this context, be regarded as appeals to human beings to look inward in order to regain connection with their own nature, which the animals have not lost. The last paragraph of the text, in the words of the gandharva, comprises the message of the story:

> Animals are still close to Nature. That is why they made noises when they saw me in the zoo. Man is destroying himself by ruining Nature. Some time back, a scholar asked me a question: What do you think about us humans? This was my answer: I have not seen more ignorant beings anywhere else. I'll say the same to my people, the gandharvas.

The gandharva describes humans as 'ignorant'. In this context, the wonder motif of the story becomes relevant. Wonder is the only means by which the attention of the child, as well as of the ignorant adult, can be attracted. It is god's way of preparing man to receive instruction.

The Poet in Society: The Author Representing Himself

The story of the gandharva also has an allegorical meaning as the autobiography of Satyanarayana. He often described himself as the incarnation of Brahminic learning. In the preface to his *Rāmāyaṇa Kalpavṛkṣhamu*, he calls himself the 'personification of the goddess of learning', a *brahmīmayamūrti*. In *Dindukinda Pokacĕkka* (*Betel nut under the Pillow*), a novel he wrote a few years before his death, there is a description of a writer, summarized here, which reflects his self-image:

> Five thousand years from now a great writer will be born among the Andhras. He will be a devotee of Siva and Visnu and will know the *brahman*, the ultimate reality. He will be a master of words. He will direct all his anger against the enemies of dharma. The powers of Kali, the age of untruth, will not be able to affect him much.[1]

The author's self-image, then, is that he is a descendent of the ancient Brahminic *ṛṣis*, sages, trapped in a society which is quickly deteriorating under the influence of Kali. In other words, he is a gandharva who has temporarily lost his wings.

Satyanarayana conveys throughout his work a deep commitment to the value of the Brahminic order of society with its varna hierarchy and the infallibility of its law books, the *Dharmashastras*. Throughout his writing he presents a society that has fallen from the supreme heights of Brahminic law to the abysmal depths of Western lawlessness. Since the publication of his novel, *Veyi Paḍagalu* (*A Thousand Hoods*), in which he supported all Hindu traditions—including traditional monarchy and varna hierarchy—severe criticism has been lodged against him by the modern, English-educated literary establishment.

What was problematic however, as discussed in the introduction, was that Satyanarayana was not easy to categorize. He wrote in modern genres but in an archaic dialect; he shared modern themes with the new poets but he defended the traditional order; his sensibilities were modern but he spoke the language of classical poets.

Satyanarayana's work was criticized as being full of inconsistencies. He was not traditional enough for the group of Sanskrit pandits who strictly wrote in the old style according to the prescriptive code of poetics, *Alamkāra śāstra*, and the code of the old grammar, *Vyākaraṇa śāstra*. This, because he too often broke the rules, and his works were replete with *doshas*, 'blemishes'. He was not modern enough for the new poets because he considered ancient Sanskrit sastras and classical poets as his ideal models and advocated a 'Back to the Vedic Age' philosophy, despising everything Western as deterioration. The modern poets attacked him as a *chāndasa*, 'old-fashioned', and ridiculed his outdated ideas, while the traditionalists rejected him for his modernisms, grammatical errors, unconventional expressions and inaccurate use of the grammar.

Neither horse nor man, this horse-man remained a source of controversy. Very much like the gandharva in

Trafalgar Square, Satyanarayana was subjected to crude investigation and inelegant exposition. In the literary context of the time, his presence was not only enigmatic, but it was even something of a problem in that he was seen as a threat to the quiet existence of the two clearly divided literary clans, traditional and modern, who knew where they stood in relation to each other. Opposing each other as routine, they still operated in their respective fields with considerable security.

Who counted as a writer and who did not was determined by the standards which were being applied. For the traditionalists, writers dating from the eleventh century represented eternal standards, standards unapproachable for contemporary writers. Since the golden age, standards had lowered with time and literature had grown 'thinner than water'. On the other hand, the modernists felt that poetry had its beginning with the new poets. The old poets did not qualify for the status of literary men. Between these two extremes existed a few intermediate positions, but the dividing lines were never confused.

The threat of Satyanarayana, who belonged to neither category, was all the greater because of his intense creative energy and his prolific literary productivity. Many 'guns' were aimed at him, and many 'prison doors' were slammed on him until he resisted the attacks with aggressive wit and more significantly with his scholarship and creativity. The traditionalists soon perceived the value of his message for them and gathered around him. Handsome tributes were paid to him for his literary excellence and scholarship, comparing him to the great writers of the past. He was called *kavisamrāṭ*, 'King of Poets'. Awards and prizes were conferred upon him. The greatest honour awarded him was the national Jnanpith Award. Like the gandharva, he was eventually welcomed as the guest of honour by the House of Lords.

All honours aside, Satyanarayana continues to be discussed in terms of traditionalism and modernism, Brahminical views and liberal ideas, in other words, 'horses and human beings'. The complexity of his works is overlooked in the controversial atmosphere of accusations and counter-accusations in which both sides concentrate on formulaic evaluations for apportioning praise or blame. The gandharva remains unrecognized as scientists and scholars argue whether he is an animal or a man.

In Vedic mythology, the gandharva is, among many other things, the mediator of poetry. In epic mythology, he is the celestial musician who lives in the sky. Mythological images confirm the gandharva as representative of poetry and assert his role in the story as the archetype of the poet. One needs only to take a brief look at the lives of great poets to realize that they ran the gauntlet of contemporary opinion. Misunderstood by readers, ill-treated by critics and often persecuted by governments, a great writer is often like the gandharva in Trafalgar Square. Many parallels between them come to one's mind as one reads the story. Some of these parallels are presented below:

The poet does not have a name until the reviewers recognize him as a poet.

The gandharva forgets his name until the scholars remind him of it. They later shorten it to Ha Hu, which then becomes popular.

The poet is known to the public when the mass media pays attention to his unconventional lifestyle.

The newspapers all over Europe publish 'strange' news about Ha Ha Hu Hu, the horse-man who speaks Sanskrit. The reports bring visitors and scientists to the gandharva.

Critics proceed with their tools to classify the poet in the accepted slots of intellectual categories.

The scientists attempt to cut the gandharva's body to investigate whether he is a man or an animal.

When the established powers consider the poet dangerous to their security, they either try to shut him up or to buy him off.

The London police imprison the gandharva when they fear harm from him. Later, when they realize that he is too strong to be imprisoned, the government tries to honour him as a guest.

The poet is free when he can fly on the power of his own creativity.

The gandharva grows his wings through powers of meditation and flies away making music.

Apparently there is an underlying pattern that reproduces a poet's biography in the way the gandharva is treated in London.

Vishnu Sharma Learns English

If the locale of *Ha Ha Hu Hu* is London, the capital of the British Empire, known to most Indians only in their fantasies and dreams, the second novella, *Vishnu Sharma Learns English*, is located close to home in Vijayawada, a dusty town in the 1960s on the banks of the Krishna river in Andhra Pradesh. The land around Vijayawada is fertile on account of a dam built by Sir Arthur Cotton, a Yorkshire engineer in the service of the English East India Company. The town also hosts a modern-style four-year college, where every subject except Telugu is taught in English.

By the time he was writing *Vishnu Sharma Learns English*, Satyanarayana's understanding of the impact of colonialism had deepened. If in *Ha Ha Hu Hu*, he was adopting the well-known nationalist position that India is spiritually superior to the material West, in writing *Vishnu Sharma Learns English*, his understanding had matured. He knew that the impact of colonialism had deeply destroyed the very basis of Indian culture, including the one called spiritual.

High culture in any country is easy to destroy; if two or three generations of scholars, poets and artists are not supported, it deteriorates. Ever since English became the language of administration and education in India, literary patronage, which poets had enjoyed during the time of the pre-colonial kings and later under the zamindars, had gradually waned. Pandits lived a meagre life and wished they had been educated in English, which would give them jobs of higher status and a better salary.

When the universities started giving MA degrees in Telugu, a new breed of scholars, who had a smattering of English and a postgraduate degree in Telugu, started turning up. They now occupied the better-paid lecturer positions in colleges. An absurd situation arose with lesser-paid scholars who had solid learning in classical Telugu and Sanskrit, and better-paid lecturers whose scholarship was shaky, teaching in the same department. A few major scholars reluctantly studied for an MA degree to qualify themselves for a lecturer position in colleges (Satyanarayana was one of them). Several scholars still held to their tradition. They did not learn English because it deviated from their tradition and so they remained outside the academy.

At one point of time, there were more scholars unemployed outside the academy than employed inside of it. The old scholars talked of their Vyākaraṇa, Alamkāra śāstra, Mimāmsa, Tarka and Vedānta, while the new scholars talked of philology, history of literature, literary criticism and linguistics, based on poorly grasped Western methods. The old scholars spoke Sanskrit and the new ones spoke English. One did not know the other's language, nor did they understand the other's concepts; they operated in parallel universes, both equally fragile and inadequate to serve the present. The old-style Sanskrit scholars lost their creativity, their ability to change with the times and address new challenges, while the new scholars educated in English were little more than parrots repeating poorly understood Western concepts. Great Sanskrit scholars of earlier generations, known for their originality and legendary control of their knowledge, were marginalized, while the best minds among the younger generation migrated into English studies, leaving the field of Sanskrit to be occupied by lesser minds that had no chance of succeeding in the new subjects taught in Western-style schools.

The protagonist of *Vishnu Sharma Learns English* is a Telugu lecturer in one of the local colleges. He has passed his MA and acquired the necessary qualification to teach Telugu. Yet, his training did not make him a scholar anywhere comparable to the traditional pandits who knew their texts inside out and were authentic representatives of their scholarly tradition. The newly trained Telugu lecturer in an English college is lost to both cultures: he wants to be like the old pandits he admires, but is afraid to reveal his ignorance before them. He is not learned enough in the Western subjects to mingle with the better-trained English scholars and scientists. He knows just enough English to get by in a modern college and respond to its administrative needs, but not enough to efficiently teach the language to his visitors from heaven. He knows a bit of the methods of Western philology, history and literary criticism, but does not know them well enough to compare them with classical Indian scholarship. Neither rooted in his own tradition, nor fully at home in the adopted one, he is a pathetic mix of the postcolonial and precolonial. He swears by the English and German scholars of Sanskrit while arguing with the traditional scholars around him, but at the same time wants to stand up for the greatness of ancient Indian culture when he faces the English-educated moderns.

In fact, this Telugu lecturer doesn't know Sanskrit well enough to teach old Telugu texts, which have a number of Sanskrit words in them and has to consult his Sanskrit-knowing pandit-colleagues to get their meanings, but he pretends to be a scholar of both Sanskrit and Telugu when he encounters the moderns, who know neither. When his unexpected guests visiting from heaven quote a line from Valmiki's Ramayana comparing Sita, who was emaciated in captivity, to the learning of a student who studies on the first day of the moon, he doesn't understand the Sanskrit quotation but pretends he does until he can piece together its meaning from their conversation. He tries to authentically represent what he romantically believes to be the greatness of Indian learning, but in the end represents only a confused generation of Indian intellectuals of his time. His personal life lies somewhere between the old and the new as well. His wife is a traditional woman, uneducated in modern ways, who cooks and takes care of the children, but at the same time drinks coffee and loves to go to the movies with her husband—two symbols of modernity. His children are going to an English school, while he himself still observes traditional rituals like the annual death ceremonies of his deceased parents, even though he occasionally skimps on details and substitutes pre-packed betel leaves rather than offering fresh ones to the Brahmins. He believes that people from heaven could come to visit him, and has great respect for the scholarship of both Vishnu Sharma and Tikkanna. At the same time, he is scared of losing his job if he openly admits their presence in his house. He has to test the waters and make sure his theosophist principal approves of the idea of a visitor from another world before he announces the news to the rest of the faculty and students. Theosophy, being a Western form of religion which incorporates Hindu ideas and mythology, legitimizes his own beliefs.

In contrast, the visitors from heaven, Tikkanna and Vishnu Sharma, understand the violence colonial learning has done to India's foundations of knowledge. One significant item of colonial learning is literary history. Literary scholars of India accepted without complaint the view that India lacked a sense of history. Problems posed by the lack of literary history present themselves even in heaven at the court of Indra, the king of gods. Indra is troubled by the questions raised by the recent visitors from earth, who did a few good things during their life on earth and earned a temporary right to enjoy the comforts of heaven. To present the conflict between colonial knowledge and traditional learning, Satyanarayana uses the Hindu religious belief that people go to heaven after their death as a reward for their good deeds, but return to earth to suffer the pain of life as soon as the merit they had earned was spent.

The issue at hand is whether Vishnu Sharma is the author of the *Pancatantra*. Vishnu Sharma lives in heaven for the merit of having been a great scholar and a writer of one of the great books on statecraft in Sanskrit. The new visitors from earth dispute his authorship. Could he show evidence that he wrote it? Any manuscript written in his own hand? Does he have any evidence that he is really who he claims to be, Vishnu Sharma? Any school records? (In colonial India such records served as identity cards issued by the state and included the date of birth and physical marks of identification such as birthmarks.) But Vishnu Sharma does not have any such records; he never went to school. His education, like that of any traditional scholar, was with a guru who taught him by word of mouth. He does not even know how to write. He dictated his text to a scribe, very much like Satyanarayana did. In narrating this debate in heaven, Satyanarayana quietly shows how the colonial state colonized individual lives, gave them a new identity and managed their minds.

Indra himself is unable to decide on the question of authorship, so he asks if there is anyone who can testify in this case. Cinnaya Suri, who happens to be in heaven, is called. He is the author of a grammar of Telugu, one that traditional scholars regard as the most authoritative. He also translated two chapters of Vishnu Sharma's *Pancatantra* into mellifluous Telugu. But he is not acceptable as a witness to the modernists who reject his grammar and his literary style along with it. (I discuss the style disputes in Telugu later in this essay.) So, Viresalingam is called to witness. He is the famous social reformer who argued that Hindu society is decadent and lost in ignorance and superstition. He accepted many of the ideas colonial scholar-administrators held about India. He comes and testifies to the effect that in all likelihood Vishnu Sharma never existed, and that the stories of the *Pancatantra* were adopted from Greek sources by some anonymous authors.

In the short presentation of this incident in heaven, Satyanarayana hints at the vast distance between what is called modern knowledge among the Indian literary community and pre-British Indian knowledge. Vishnu Sharma unpretentiously articulates the violence done by Western philology and the Western concept of a 'text' to Indian literary culture.

The focus of the novella, however, is on the way English is taught to Indian children. Satyanarayana uses the naive expectation of the heavenly visitors that English is structured like Sanskrit. They learn the alphabet and want to read a book right away. They expect alphabets and syntax of all languages to work like Sanskrit. The instructor, who is himself not a trained teacher of English as a foreign language, makes a mess of his teaching. Unable to distinguish between a language and the script in which it is written, and to explain the difference between alphabetic and syllabic writing systems, the instructor confuses the heavenly visitors. Consequently, silly arguments about spelling give rise to cheap shots against English. Instruction degenerates into desultory banter, while the students from heaven find fault with English and denounce it as an uncivilized language. But through all this talk, one point comes through—the instructor is utterly incompetent to teach English and only succeeds in giving a wrong picture of the language.

Strategically using the incompetence of the modern Telugu lecturer to teach the heavenly visitors English, Satyanarayana shows that while Sanskrit could be taught to those who know Indian languages by teaching them morphological rules that constitute noun declensions and verb forms, this method does not work in teaching English. In English, syntax has a greater role to play than morphology, and its phonology is not transparent in its orthography. Furthermore, the semantic world of English is vastly different from any Indian language. Indian languages, as has been shown by linguists, share a semantic-syntactic substratum and differ mostly at the level of morphology.[2] Native speakers of an Indian language quickly learn that the morphemes of another Indian language are organized in very much the same way as their own language. Most of what one has to learn is vocabulary, and of course the script. What is usually called grammar is somewhat minimal and semantics does not pose much of a problem. The influence of historical and comparative linguistics dividing Indian languages into separate families, particularly Indo-Aryan and Dravidian, popularly misunderstood, drove a wedge between one group of Indian languages and the other.

Satyanarayana understands that all Indian languages share a syntactic-semantic base. He uses the naivete of the visitors from heaven strategically to show that English fundamentally transforms the syntax and semantics of Indian culture—unlike Sanskrit, Persian or Arabic. What Tikkanna says jokingly about the English sentence 'Rama killed Ravana' has a deeper and more profound meaning. This is how the conversation goes: Tikkanna asks for an English translation of a Telugu sentence, *rāmuḍu rāvaṇuni campĕnu*. (Literally: Rama Ravana [accusative] killed). Telugu being an SOV language, the verb comes at the end. In English it is 'Rama killed Ravana'. (English being an SVO language, the verb comes in the middle and the object at the end.)

Tikkanna says, 'I see, but why did you put killed in the middle? The one who is to be killed is free to escape if he is at the very end of the sentence.' The Telugu lecturer doesn't understand, the joke. Tikkanna explains: 'You say "Rama killed" but as soon as you say kill, suppose Ravana ran away, who is left to be killed? You have to bring a dog or a goat in his place. But suppose you have Ravana already in the sentence before you utter the verb, he is stuck, he can't go anywhere; he *has* to die.'

Contrary to what is commonly understood by many readers of this novella,[3] Satyanarayana is not making fun of the English language as such; he is making a point about the unsuitability of the present methods of teaching English to Indian children. They get confused, but silently suffer, because they cannot complain. The few who learn it well can speak it almost as if it were their mother tongue; sometimes, depending on the depth of their interaction with it, they even forget their native tongue and its literature almost completely.

English is overwritten on their minds and permeates their
unconscious, erasing the structure of their cognitive world.
Successful Indo-Anglican writers from Anita Desai to
Salman Rushdie, from Vikram Seth to Jhumpa Lahiri are
barely competent in Indian languages, if they ever grew up in
one. Satyanarayana passionately believes that the reason for
the success of the colonial project consists in infiltrating into
the Indian mind—not to interact with it and energize it, but
to trample on it and trash it. Admittedly, Satyanarayana is an
extremist in his anti-colonial position. But even from the more
balanced perspective of contemporary cultural historians, the
chasm between the postcolonial and the precolonial in India's
culture is vast. The subaltern historians who made a valiant
effort to write Indian history from below agree.

To quote Dipesh Chakrabarty again:

> Faced with the task of analyzing developments or social
> practices in modern India, few if any Indian social scientists
> or social scientists of India would argue seriously with,
> say, the thirteenth-century logician Gangesa or with
> the grammarian and linguistic philosopher Bartrihari
> (fifth to sixth centuries), or with the tenth or eleventh-
> century aesthetician Abhinavagupta . . . They treat these
> traditions as truly dead, as history.[4]

A similar sentiment is expressed in Satyanarayana's 1930
novel *Veyi Paḍagalu (A Thousand Hoods)* in which a
character says, 'I bet that in ten years there would be no
one around who can call himself a *bhashayānta vaiyākaraṇi*

or a *bādhānta tārkika'*, referring to scholars of grammar and logic.[5]

The Dream

Finally, there is the dream, the frame of the narrative of *Vishnu*. It is a dream that occurs serially, as the author sleeps. The reader almost loses their way into the narrative happening inside the dream, but wakes up to realize that it is a dream by the occasional reminders that the author is narrating his dream. The reader may wonder whether the author is actually narrating the dream as it progresses or if the novella is a recollection after the dream has ended. The experiential fact is that the reader does not feel they are reading the text—they are listening to the narrative as the author tells it while it is occurring. This experience is created by the nature of the sentences and the narrative style. The novella *tells* the story; the reader *listens* to the author/dreamer as he tells it. The fact that it is a written text and that you are reading it is erased from memory, even as you read it.

Dreams are not new to Telugu literature. One of the very first poets, Tikkanna of the eleventh century, tells how God Hari-hara-natha, a composite form of Siva and Vishnu, appears to him in his dream and tells him to write the Mahabharata. King Krishnadevaraya of the sixteenth century narrates an elaborate dream in which Vishnu appears and tells the king to compose *Āmuktamālyada* in Telugu. The God even gives the theme, the language in which the poem has to be written, and to whom it should be dedicated.

These are dreams that the dreamers/authors tell us after they wake up. Satyanarayana's dream is different: it is narrated as it is happening, so the reader participates in the dream while listening to it. The reader wakes up when the dreamer wakes up and dreams when the dreamer dreams. The reader follows the dream time without even being aware of it. The events of the dream take several days, even months, but the worldly time of the dream is hardly a few hours. The shift in time from dream to reality is so uneventful that despite being awakened periodically, the flow of time is smooth. Looking back after finishing the novel, the reader may wonder what is actually real and what is a dream.

Magical Realism?

Satyanarayana wrote the first of these novellas, *Ha Ha Hu Hu*, long before magical realism came into literary critical discourse. By the time he wrote *Vishnu*, the term was popular, but not in Telugu literary criticism. One of García Márquez's stories, 'A Very Old Man with Enormous Wings', bears extraordinary similarities with *Ha Ha Hu Hu*. It is very unlikely that Satyanarayana read García Márquez, nor is it likely that García Márquez read the Telugu story. If the similarities are accidental, they are still amazing.

Satyanarayana was aware he was creating a new technique of writing a novel but did not give it a name. The technique is strategic, intended to make the idea strikingly clear. The reader is asked to suspend their judgement and accept that gandharvas can fall into the centre of an industrial city, that dead people from heaven can visit the earth and that dreams can occur serially. If the reader can give in to these concessions ungrudgingly, the rest of the narrative feels as realistic as in any other novel. The author gains a certain degree of freedom from the restrictions of realism. The reader can have their fancy run as wild as they wish—all in a realistic frame. And unlike García Márquez, or for that matter Salman Rushdie, Satyanarayana has an added advantage. His Hindu mythological world allows these concessions as normal events. Hindus do believe at one level that gandharvas exist and that they speak Sanskrit, and that good people go to heaven and can visit earth, so that the author's dream does not sound all that outlandish.

Conclusion

Almost seventy years after the British have left India, memories of colonial rule have all but faded, but in a strange twist of history, the cultural and institutional foundations of the colonial rule continue. English, which during the freedom movement, was expected to be replaced by an Indian national language has only become stronger after the British left. English has become the path to enter the middle class. It's not the income, property or family status that makes a person respected as middle class; it is English. The lower classes are willing to spend money to give an English education to their children, even denying minimum comforts for themselves. Dalit communities demand that their children be sent to English-medium schools, where all the rich kids go.

In a context such as this, the novellas of this book could have a somewhat difficult reception, misunderstood as some kind of a call for Brahmin superiority, or a return to a Vedic past.

A moment of thoughtful reflection would lead to the deeper meaning of the novellas. Colonialism did not conquer India militarily, though considerable violence was used by the British to subdue the Indians who opposed them. Colonial practices attacked Indian self-confidence, so the colonized people looked for the acceptance, approval and recognition of the colonial master culture. They wilfully surrendered and became subservient. What a colonized culture lost was not its political independence alone, and as history showed, it was regained. But its creative energies of centuries were lost. The nation that emerged from the onslaught of colonialism became unknowingly derivative. Loss of one's own language of creative thinking was the ultimate loss.

Satyanarayana recognizes that colonialism erased the basic foundation of the Indian mind and colonized its consciousness. Everything that the most ardent nationalists think they are recovering in the name of religion, history, society and culture is derived from the categories that colonialism had taught them. In contrast, reclaiming the forgotten foundations of precolonial Indian thought and feeling is what Satyanarayana's project undertakes. From this perspective, the two novellas are indeed revolutionary.

Endnotes

Introduction

1. Dipesh Chakrabarty, *Provincializing Europe*, Princeton: Princeton University Press, 2000, p. 4.

2. For more about Venkata Sastry, see my *Hibiscus on the Lake: Twentieth-Century Telugu Poetry from India*, Madison, WI: University of Wisconsin Press, 2003, pp. 245–46; or *Twentieth Century Telugu Poetry: An Anthology*, New Delhi: Oxford University Press, 2002, pp. 293–95; and my 'Buddhism in Modern Andhra: Literary Representations from Telugu', *Journal of Hindu Studies*, 2008: 1:93–119 reprinted in my *Text and Tradition in South India*, Ranikhet: Permanent Black, 2016, pp. 361–96.

3. There was yet another group of pandits who were trained by individual gurus and who did not accept the standards of Oriental colleges established by the colonial government. But they were considered unqualified to be employed in schools and colleges because they did not have recognized diplomas.

4. Quote by Bhamidipati Kameswara Rao, in his essay 'Rĕndo bhāsha meṣṭaru', in *Mana Tĕlugu*.

5. See Kottapalli Virabhadra Rao, *Telugu Sāhityamupai Inglīshu Prabhāvamu*, Second enlarged edition, Secunderabad: 1986, p. 415.

6. Bhamidipati Kameswara Rao, *Mana Tělugu*, Rajamahendravaram: Saraswati Power Press, 1948, pp. 65–88.

7. Linguist Ganti Jogi Somayaji notes this in his *Āndhra Bhāshāvikāsamu*, Author: Machilipatnam, 1968 (1947), p. 590.

8. A number of new institutions in the private sector that were built around this time all carried Andhra as part of their name. Among them, organizations such as Andhra Mahasabha and Krishnadevaraya Andhra Bhasha Nilayamu in the princely state of Hyderabad reflected the democratic aspirations of the Telugu people against the rule of the Nizam. The daily paper *Āndhra Patrika* in Madras (now Chennai) reflected Telugu cultural identity in the composite state of Madras. Andhra Bank and Andhra Scientific Company were expressions of Telugu patriotism in the private business sector. And Andhra University in Visakhapatnam stood as a major expression of the aspirations of the Telugu people for recognition of their desire for a separate state.

9. The English were called hūnas by the pandits of the time.

10. Chellapilla Venkata Sastry, *Kāmeśvarī Śatakamu*, Chitrada: Ramavilasa Press, 1925, verse 22.

11. Viswanadha Satyanarayana, *Venarāju*, in *Viśwanāthavāri Paurāṇika Nāṭakamula Sumpuṭi*, Vijayawada: Sri Viswanadha Publications, 2007, p. 219.

12. Viswanadha Satyanarayana *Rāmāyaṇa Kalpavṛkshamu*, Vol. 1, 'Preface'. Translation in collaboration with David Shulman.

13. There were a few literary journals in Telugu of which *Bhārati* was well known, but daily newspapers such as *Āndhra Patrika* gave prominent attention to literary matters as well.

14. For instance, a cartoon by a popular artist, Bapu, depicts an old man with a pen in his hand, dressed like a Brahmin, who tells his wife as she is chopping vegetables in the kitchen: 'Look, I am writing the Ramayana.' She responds: 'Stop boasting. You can get it easily from the bookstore.'

15. Narayana Rao and Shulman, *A Poem at the Right Moment*, Berkeley: University of California Press, 1998, p. 51.

16. According to a popular concept from the *Alamkāra* tradition of literary theory, textures in literary texts are of three kinds. One is the grape texture, *drākshā-pāka*. A poem written in this texture is easily accessible to you and you enjoy it as you read with no effort—like you taste grapes. The second is the banana texture, *kadaḷī-pāka*, where you have to make an effort to understand the poem, like peeling the outer skin of a banana before you can enjoy the fruit. The third is the coconut texture, *nārikeḷa-pāka*, where you have to work hard to get the beauty of the poem, because the style is hard and you need to consult dictionaries to understand the words— just as you have to tear off the fibrous shell and break the inner nut before you get to taste the meat of a coconut. Continuing this analogy, Rukmininatha Sastri implies that Satyanarayana's poems are in rock-texture, *pāshāṇa-pāka*; you have to work really hard to break the rock and even then you get nothing out of it.

17. Narayana Rao and Shulman. Ibid. p. 50.

18. 'Rēṇḍu nakshatrālu', in *Andhra Bhūruti*, 1.5, Machilipatnam, 20 August 1926. Also included in *Bhrashṭa Yogi, Khaṇḍa-kāvya Sampuṭi* 1, Vijayawada: V.S.N. & Co., 2000, p. 24. The context of reading these verses is told by Kovela Sampatkumaracharya in his *Viśvanātha Satyanārāyaṇa*, New Delhi: Sahitya Akademi, 2007, pp. 126–27. Sampatkumaracharya, however, says that the reward offered by the maharaja was 1116 rupees.

19. Stories are told that the raja of Challapalli, a zamindar in Krishna district, offered to pay for printing Satyanarayana's *Rāmāyaṇa Kalpavṛkshamu*, but did not keep his word after the first volume. The entire *Rāmāyaṇa* is written as if the raja of Challapalli is the listener, invoking him in the beginning and at the end of every chapter. However, the description of his family in the preface is removed from the later editions of the book, and a few more listeners added as well.

20. See Velcheru Narayana Rao, *Twentieth Century Telugu Poetry: An Anthology*, New Delhi: Oxford University Press, 2002. American edition: *Hibiscus on the Lake: Twentieth-Century Telugu Poetry from India*, Madison, Wi: The University of Wisconsin Press, 2003.

21. *Viśvanāthavāṅgmayasūcika* (Bibliography of Viswanadha's works), Ketavrapu Venkata Ramakoti Sastri and Kovela Suprasannacharyulu (eds), Warrangal: Telugu Department, Postgraduate Centre, 1974, gives 1932 as the date of its composition, but Satyanarayana's son Pavani Sastri gives 1952 in *Ha Ha Hu Hu* (Vijayawada: Sri Viswanadha Publications, 2006). The discrepancy needs more research to resolve.

Ha Ha Hu Hu

1. The religious mark worn by Vaishnavas among Hindus.

2. Police in London do not bear arms. The author probably realized it halfway through and began to use 'soldiers' as well from page 49. However, soldiers do not take orders from the Mayor, a detail lost on the author.

3. This is Prakrit. Its Sanskrit equivalent is, *Kim gatosmi*. 'What happened to me?'

4. Sanskrit equivalent: *Aho me adhanyatvam. Kim etat? Kim samādiṣṭah?* 'What a misfortune! What is this? What has happened?'

5. Sanskrit equivalent: *Konu tvam?* 'Who are you?'

6. A round, copper vessel for drinking water.

7. Sanskrit equivalent: *Kim mayā atra śrutam? Kim idam?* 'What have I heard? What is this?'

8. Sanskrit equivalent: *Pṛcchiṣyāmi. Asti vā atra nadī?* 'Pray, tell me, is there a river nearby?'

9. Same as No. 8.

10. 'What did you say?'

11. 'Is there a river nearby? I want to take a bath.'

12. 'Yes, of course.'

13. The original includes the following dialogue: Sanskrit Scholar: 'But the wounds that we'd make wouldn't heal with all our medicine. The only result of the experiment might be the wounds on his head.' I removed these lines because they are out of context and seem to be included here by mistake.

14. 'Where's the chief?'

15. 'All languages came from Sanskrit. What is there to investigate?'

16. 'Please ask.'

17. Tapas indicates austerity and severe discipline of the body and mind that generates heat. It is used in many meanings, including an act of generating heat that could destroy the world, if gods do not attend to the demands of the person performing tapas. Here it is used in its milder meaning indicating a deep meditation to see the truth.

18. 'How petty humans can be!'

Vishnu Sharma Learns English

1. A ritual, usually called sacrifice, involves a number of specially trained Brahmins who perform chants from the Vedas. All of them need to be paid and fed. The sacrifice is therefore expensive. The person who performs a sacrifice is called Somayāji.

2. Readers would note that Tikkanna already sat down on
    page 67. An inconsistency in the original, apparently because
    Satyanarayana was dictating and did not check back.

3. A major issue in modern Telugu literary taste. Vemanna,
    of an unknown date, but generally believed to belong to
    the seventeenth century, who wrote an unknown number
    of simple verses making statements about society, ritual
    habits and women, was vehemently anti-Brahmanical. Many
    modern critics consider him a social revolutionary and a
    great poet. Sri Sri, the influential Marxist poet, included him
    among the three great poets of Telugu literature.

4. Popularly considered the first modern poet in Telugu. I
    translated his famous play *Kanyśulkam*. See, Gurajada Apparao,
    Girls for Sale: Kanyasulkam, a Play from Colonial India, New
    Delhi: Penguin India, 2011. American edition, published by
    Bloomington IN: Indiana University Press, 2007.

5. Reference here is to the mythological plays popular during
    the first half of the twentieth century, where many popular
    actors were asked by the audience to sing a verse or a song
    for which they were known. The audience often yelled 'once
    more' to demand a repeat performance. It was immaterial
    whether the verse/song was related to the play or not.

6. Tikkanna writes the story of his dream in the preface to his
    Telugu Mahabharata. According to this, God Hari-hara-
    natha, a composite form of Vishnu and Siva, appears in
    Tikkanna's dream and asks him to write the Mahabharata
    in Telugu.

Afterword

1. *Diṇḍu krindi poka cĕkka*, Vijayawada: Sri Viswanatha
    Publications, Third Edition, 2006 (First edition 1967),
    summarized from page 194.

2. For a more detailed discussion on this see, Colin P. Masica, *Defining a Linguistic Area: South Asia*, Chicago: University of Chicago Press, 1976.

3. A recent dramatization of this novella by C.S. Rao (*Vishnu Sharma Inglīshu Caduvu: Naṭakīkaraṇa*, Kakinada: Ramani Pracuranalu, 2010), is one example of how this novella is read as a satire on the English language.

4. Dipesh Chakrabarty, *Provincializing Europe*. Ibid. pp. 5–6.

5. A scholar of grammar who studied the *Mahābhāshya*, the great commentary by Patanjali, is called a *bhāshyānta vayyākaraṇi*, and a logician who mastered how to refute a pseudo argument, *Bādha*, is called a *bādhānta tārkika*.

Acknowledgements

I translated *Ha Ha Hu Hu* some twenty years ago.

It was sitting on my computer all along. I shared it with several of my friends, including Sanjay Subrahmanyam and Kirin Narayan. Many of their comments and suggestions were useful to me.

I was not able to find a publisher for a volume so small, and abandoned the idea of publishing it.

After some years, I translated *Vishnu Sharma Inglishu Caduvu* and hoped that together the two novellas would make a volume with my introduction and afterword. I kept on improving my translation and gathered several versions on my computer.

Two friends, Joyce Flueckiger and Sylvia Dakessian, came to my rescue when I was not sure which of the several versions I should send to the publisher. With their active assistance, I picked one version and finalized it for publication.

I am truly grateful to Rachna Pratap at Penguin, who patiently suffered through the initial stages of creating a contract. I am especially thankful to Ambar Sahil Chatterjee, my editor, for his gentle and thoughtful decisions, and Paloma Dutta for her efficient copy editing. Most importantly, I am grateful to Viswanadha Satyanarayana, the author's grandson, for gracefully giving me copyright to publish my translations.

Venkateswara Rao Veluri has been my friend from our Eluru days of the 1960s along with Penmetsha Suryanarayana Raju, whom we called Raju, and Ponangi Ramakrishna Rao (P.R.K. Rao). We read a number of books together and talked a lot about each author late into the night. Their company made my education in European literature exciting. Venkateswara Rao's friendship continued after I came to the US, and over the last several decades we read and argued. Trained in nuclear physics, he introduced me to the mysteries of the intersection of poetry and physics. I learned interesting new ideas every time I talked to him.

I dedicate this book to Venkateswara Rao and his wife Shanti who made my life in Atlanta truly enjoyable.

I am glad my translations are seeing the light of day after many years of hibernation.

Atlanta, 2018   VNR